DEATH
OF A
PATRIOT

by

, GD

as told to Helen Games, MBA, who
translated the story to the author Ben R. Games, PhD.

DEATH OF A PATRIOT

© Copyright 2010 Ben R. Games, PhD

ALL RIGHTS RESERVED

www.FideliPublishing.com

ISBN: 978-1-60414-184-9

DEDICATED TO

All the Patriots of these
Caribbean Islands
who are working together making
JAGS McCartney's dream
come true.

May the people always remember that these islands
belong to God and were saved for his people.
When the Slave Traders threw the sick and lame
overboard they had nothing, and still the
people were given God's greatest gift ...

the TURKS & CAICOS ISLANDS

Story told by Montana, GD,
Chief of Security
of
The Games Clan

Montana, GD

DEATH OF A PATRIOT
by BEN R. GAMES, PhD

Author's Statement

Facts

Prologue

Montana's Dream

Told by Montana, GD, to Helen Games, MBA,
& written by Ben Games, PhD.

Published by Fideli Publishing Inc;
Historical Documents by: Ben R. Games, Jr, (Bud) AS,
and "Super C" of GDT.

.

STATEMENT

All service dogs form a special bond with the person who
is their companion. Montana is a male, ninety-pound black
Labrador Retriever who has formed this type of relationship

with my wife, Helen. I believe that he actually tries to communicate with his mind by staring into her eyes. After watching him work, it is easy to think that he may have telepathic ability.

This story is semi-biographical but maybe it's the way Montana would tell about an adventure in his dreams. Like any story that is told to one person and then to another, things may not have happened exactly as I wrote it. The country, towns, people, and Montana's clan are real, but the animals in the story are figments in a dog's dream.

Montana likes people-puppies and treats adults with dignity and respect. When he meets other people with dogs, he comes to attention acting as if they were special. From the way he performs, it is easy to understand that he must think the people who don't have a dog are the handicapped ones. I think he is right.

— *Ben R. Games, PhD*

PATRIOT FACTS

The author is a member of the "Games Clan" and believes that everyone has a story to tell. Keeping a journal or diary will document the story and form the building blocks needed for a window that looks into the future. What has happened in the past can happen again unless a change in the pattern of things is made. Some have tried to change history by rewriting it, but this never works. History must be lived, and today is tomorrow's history. To help make this happen, the author started publishing stories based upon his Journals. **That's a FACT.**

Death Of A Patriot is a semi-biographical story. When the author wrote his autobiography at the request of the US Army Historical Library, he found that it would take more than one book to cover everything he'd done and seen in his life. There are many stories of the Games Clan's adventures that are part of this history. The pictures and documents in the Historical Chapter show what really happened. **That's a FACT.**

The author's wife, Helen, is encouraging him to write another book in his autobiographical series. The author has agreed, but will create the stories as semi-biographies published under individual titles. This way those who read about the adventures can decide for themselves what parts are true and what's conjecture. Each adventure is a separate story. When put together, these stories form the true autobiography of the man born in Elkhart, Indiana, on 5 May 1924. Many of the stories start out as a dream of Helen's service dog, Montana, who is the self-appointed chief of security for the family. **That's a FACT.**

When the author refers to his family, he is including the animals who share his home. Helen's service dog, Montana, always travels with them, so they avoid countries where dogs are not welcome. In 1978, the author and his family visited the island of Grand Turk in the Turks & Caicos Islands, British West Indies. In 1980, JAGS McCartney, Chief Minister and Patriot, asked them to return to help stop the Columbian drug cartels from using the country's national airline, TCNA for the transportation of drugs. **That's a FACT.**

This story was not written to change history, but to tell how the Games Clan lived it. If someone were to write a history book about this period in the Turks & Caicos Islands, it could be called *The Islands' Drug War.* Truthfully, not all of the battles were won by the good guys. Many died during the war, one being the Patriot and Chief Minister, the Honorable JAGS McCartney. **That's a FACT.**

The people are real and the events really happened in this adventure story. Yet this tale as it's written is only a dog's dream and Montana does not always see things the way people do. If the reader was there, he or she should write in the margin of the book what they were doing when the events took place. Then when they tell someone about the story, they can say what really happened. Then, and only then, can this story become a part of the Turks & Caicos Islands' history. **That's a FACT.**

Montana is a male black Labrador Retriever who graduated from the Southeastern Guide Dog School with a degree of "GD". His grandfather's name was Freedom, and he started the school. His father's name was Vermont and his mother's name was Blizzard. When he was seven weeks old, she sent him to live with his father who started teaching him how to become a guide dog.

After two years of training, he graduated from the guide dog school and was assigned to work with Dennis, a blind detective. This is where he learned police work. During training, he learned over 40 commands, but most of all he learned about people. While in puppy training, he had a hard time understanding the word "handicap." Then one day he heard someone refer to a man in a wheelchair was being handicapped and he noticed the man didn't have a dog. That's when he decided that the word "handicap" must mean someone who does not have a dog to help him. Today guide dog trainers teach dogs to help people in wheelchairs, as well as how to help people with all types of special needs. **That's a FACT.**

While working in Denver, Colorado, with his detective partner, Montana contracted an ear infection. He returned to the Guide Dog School to recover. While on medical leave he helped people-puppies learn about guide dogs. Montana was then assigned as a companion for Helen, a lady he had bonded with when he was in puppy training. Together they traveled by boat, plane, train, and by a special RV while raising funds to help puppies attend a Guide Dog School. **That's a FACT.**

Sometimes in Montana's dreams a person is named and the author isn't sure if they are real or just part of a dog's imagination. This adventure takes place in the country known as the Turks & Caicos Islands, BWI. If you ever vacation or visit there, ask a citizen of the islands if the events Montana describes in his dream are true and really happened. You may get an answer of "Yes, that is the way it was," or "No, it is only a dog's dream." Or they may tell you the *real* story. **That's a FACT.**

Another problem the author had in writing this story was that dog and human years are different. Therefore, there is no way to fix an exact time when each event actually took place. The author wrote the story as Montana told it, from a dog's view. Montana's ability to read and send messages to other dogs is something that he likes to do. Montana must also believe that he has telepathic contact with his companion, Helen, and with other animals. **That's a FACT.**

As a member of the Games family clan, Montana is in charge of security, is guide dog trained, and the self-appointed leader of the clan. The other members include Ben, General Manager of TCNA during 1980; Helen, who is also his companion and interpreter of dog dreams; Ben and Helen's two sons, Bud, who is a chef in a Tidewell Hospice House; and Jon, who works in research and as an analyst for the US Internal Revenue Service; and last, but not least, a large, black, male cat named Smoky who protects the house from rats, lizards, and snakes.

Everyone had a job to do while helping the Turks & Caicos Islands' people in this adventure. Remember, when a story is told to one person and then repeated to another it changes a little with each telling. **That's a FACT**

The patriot in this story was JAGS McCartney, also known as just JAGS. He was leader of the PDM political party. The mystery and secrecy surrounding his assassination in 1980 has fueled rumors and many theories about what really happened. Even his friend and loyal supporter, Earl "Super C" Ingram, could only guess at some of the answers. One thing is known: At the time of his death, he was leading his country through a minefield of political intrigue and into the future.

The British Governor of the Turks & Caicos Islands during this period was the Honorable John Strong, the Police Commissioner was Stanley E. Williams, and the Manager of the TCNA was Ben R. Games, PhD. **That's a FACT.**

The Turks & Caicos Islands, British West Indies, are comprised of 40 small islands — if you count unnamed rocks sticking out of the sea. They are located 575 miles southeast of Miami, Florida. If a crow continues to fly southeast it is only another 400 miles to Puerto Rico. The island of Espanola, with Haiti and the Dominican Republic, are 100 miles south. Cuba is only 130 miles to the west, and Colombia, where the large drug cartels are located, is just 600 miles south of the Caicos Islands. In 1980, South Caicos was a refueling stop for drug planes on their way into the United States. **That's a FACT.**

There were no TV stations on the islands and there was

only one radio station. On the north end of Grand Turk, near the lighthouse, was a US Naval Station used to test surface-to-space lasers. On the South end of the island, six miles away from the naval station, was a US Air Force missile and spacecraft tracking site. On East Caicos, the US Coast Guard had a Loran "C" navigation station, and on South Caicos, the Cubans had ten acres of land with a building next to the international airport where they repacked lobster, fish, and other items produced in Cuba. The repackaged goods were then smuggled into Miami and sold as legal imports of the Turks & Caicos Islands. **That's a FACT.**

The Columbian drug cartels were trying to change South Caicos from a refueling stop for drug planes to a flea market where US drug dealers could purchase their supplies. They had established an international bank at the airport and had agreements in place for using the radio navigation systems established by the airlines. All they needed was a warehouse system like the Cubans had, and South Caicos would become the drug capital of the Caribbean. The future of the islands was in the hands of its Patriots. **That's a FACT.**

The Lord made the islands so that their highest point of land is only forty feet above the sea. He filled the beaches with white sand and surrounded the islands with a crystal-clear sea full of lobster and fish. The sun warms the land during the day, while the wind cools it at night. There are no rivers or springs, so Fuujin, the Okinawa God of Wind, sends clouds during the night to bring fresh water for the thirsty land. A night sky covers the islands with a blanket of stars turning them into shinning jewels of the Caribbean. **That's a FACT.**

The Carol "B" was an 80-foot fishing boat that was being used to smuggle cannabis (bales of marijuana) into the Turks & Caicos Islands. The pot was then loaded onto planes and flown to Florida. The vessel was located and sunk in the shallow seas of the Caicos Banks by Ben R. Games, PhD. **That's a FACT.**

God loaned the islands to a tribe of Indians. Later they were visited by a sailing ship whose sailors carried a fever and all the Indians died. Then the land waited in the sun until pirates came and started using the area as a base to hunt Spanish Gold Galleons sailing on the Caribbean Sea. Later, an English fleet came and captured the pirates. They took all the women and children to other islands and hung the men. **That's a FACT.**

Once again the island rested, waiting for the people that God had made this land for. The islands have no coal, gold, or other things that men crave. They have no forests, rushing rivers, wild beasts, mountains, or ice or snow. The sea surrounding the islands is warm, full of fish, lobster, and conch. It seems God knew of man's inhuman ways toward His other children who would someday need the land. The islands continued to lie in the sun waiting for their people to come. **That's a FACT.**

Soon the slave ships would pass the islands in the night on their way from Africa. As they silently slipped pass Grand Turk which lay just off of their starboard side, it was time to prepare the cargo of slaves for the market a few days away. In the Grand Turk Pass, the water is over 6000 feet deep with no shoals or rocks to endanger a sailing ship. The slave ships could sail within a hundred feet of the white sandy shore where the water was smooth. The light wind blew the stink of the slaves away from the ship and cooled the lower decks. These cooling winds blew out of the west toward the beaches that were long and sandy. The slave masters would pass between rows of slaves looking for the sick, weak, and dying. **That's a FACT.**

In the dark of night with the only sounds being the moans of the shackled men and women, the slave masters would strike off the chains of those who could not be sold. Then they would dispose of their human cargo by throwing them over the side of the ship. The men and women were naked, dirty, and weak from hunger. Many were sick and some had been injured by the chains and rough seas on the long voyage. As the slave masters threw them over the gunwale, they had a feeling that the fall would never stop. Most did not even cry out, because no human could help them. **That's a FACT.**

As they sank into the warm waters of the sea, it was like being baptized; they were revived, cleaned, and the salt water started to heal them. When their heads bobbed out of the water, they saw the moon lighting a long sandy beach just a few feet ahead. The salt water helped them float as the gentle wind pushed them toward the land. They crawled out of the sea upon the sand, not knowing or caring what was going to happen next. The naked men and women just lay upon their backs looking at a blanket of stars. **That's a FACT.**

As the slave ship slowly sailed past Grand Turk, the rain clouds started to hide both the ship and the moon. It was just before dawn and God's children needed fresh water to survive. Then the rains came and they were refreshed. As the sun came up, warming them, they started to sit up, and some even began to walk around looking for food. Someone looked out at the sea and cried out, "Look, the conch are everywhere!" The people waded out into the water a few feet and then reached down and found enough conch to feed everyone. The islands were happy, because their people had arrived. **That's a FACT.**

At the time of this adventure, John Houseman of Grand Turk used to tell stories about the history of the Turks & Caicos Islands over cocktails at the Salt Raker Inn while waiting for his evening meal. One tale he told was about how Count Czernin and his wife, Helen, arrived on Pine Cay via New York from the ashes of the Austro-Hungarian Empire. They built a house on Pirate Cay, and the Count would take his early morning stroll on the virgin beach which stretches some twenty miles from Whitby on North Caicos to Blue Hills on Providenciales with only four fordable cuts intervening. The Cays; Pirate, Dellis, Fort George, Pine, and Water were otherwise uninhabited. At that time, there were no roads, only trails in the Lower Caicos, and a sloop or Shank's Pony were the sole means of transport. **That's a FACT.**

A Turks & Caicos fisherman from Sandy Point beached his skiff on the wide sandy beach to knock his harvest of conch one morning. To his surprise, he was met by the elderly Count, who greeted him with a flourish of his wide-brimmed hat raised from a mane of snow-white hair and a salute with his silver-knobbed cane. Why was he surprised? The hat and cane were all that adorned the old aristocrat. **That's a FACT.**

Dogs dream while sleeping just like people. Sometimes

they give a little bark or even move their legs like they are running. Montana does this, and his companion says he is living one of his dreams. When he wakes up, he stands or sits and stares into her eyes. Maybe he is telling her about the dream and how he almost caught the rabbit. **That's a FACT.**

Like all good stories, there is a mystery about who really died when a terrorist's bomb went off and destroyed the aircraft that JAGS was traveling on in the United States. "Super C" identified the Chief Minister's body, and the FBI identified a US Democrat NJ state Chairman plus the pilot, but no one could identify the woman who died with them in the explosion. Ben thought it could have been a special KGB agent or even a CIA contract agent operating under cover. A week after the assignation of JAGS, one of Montana's cohort/agents on South Caicos reported that a man traveling on an Air Florida airliner through South Caicos to Columbia used a passport issued to James Joyce, one of the men the FBI had identified as being killed in the explosion. **That's a FACT.**

In this story, Montana is continuing with the work of establishing an intelligence network using the dogs of the Turks & Caicos Islands. JAGS McCartney, Chief Minister, had requested that the Games Clan join him on Grand Turk to help stop the movement of drugs by the cartels on TCNA planes. **That's a FACT.**

Some people believe that they have lived other lives on Earth as people or animals. Dogs may have lived other dog lives and may have come back as a Great Dane or even a Poodle to help someone they love and have bonded with. A dog's dream may be about the way he lived in a past life or when he almost caught the rabbit. **That's a FACT.**

To be accepted by the people of the Turks & Caicos Islands with all the family members including Montana as landowners with absolute title was an honor. British Governor John Strong's invitation to join the islands' celebration on the occasion of the Official Birthday Party for Her Majesty, Queen Elizabeth, at Government House on Saturday the 14th June 1980, made the Games Clan part of Turks & Caicos Islands history. **That's a FACT.**

As a member of the Board of Directors and General Manager of the national airline (TCNA) Ben was also in charge of furnishing aircraft and pilots for the national police forces. The pilots came from Brazil, Haiti, the United States, India, and the Turks & Caicos Islands. Because the pilots were not paid as policemen or soldiers, most of the drug planes they captured were flown by Ben and his chief pilot, Barkley Barron. **That's a FACT.**

Helen, who has an MBA, made the Games home in Cockburn Town on Airport Road, Grand Turk. Her education was in business, and she volunteered to assist TCNA by overseeing the Comptrollers Office of the airline while teaching accounting procedures to the employees. Ben Jr. (Bud) also volunteered to visit the US to track supplies and equipment ordered by the airline. Montana was the Chief of Security for the Clan. **That's a FACT.**

JAGS McCartney, Chief Minister, was trying to keep the United States DEA and Customs offices happy by stopping the flow of drugs through the islands to the US. At the same time, he was working to keep the British government from suspending the country's charter because of the drug cartels. All this was occurring while the Communists were trying to intervene in the US space program on Grand Turk. **That's a FACT.**

Grand Turk had a USAF down-range tracking station for missiles and NASA space missions. It was also the first land picked for an America astronaut to use when he returned from space. There was no ticker tape parade, but there were friendly people welcoming a US astronaut with conch fritters as a symbol of giving life (their ancestors ate conch to survive when they arrived in the land that God had prepared for them). To balance all this activity and at the same time fight the drug cartels seemed like an impossible task, but JAGS did it. **That's a FACT.**

JAGS had a plan to fight a secret war without an army. He thought of it as the "Islands Drug War," and called it a Police Action. This satisfied his two major allies — Great Britain and the United States. He also secretly recruited two men to act as his Generals to help fight the war. One was the Commissioner of Police, Stanley E. Williams, and the other was TCNA Manager Ben R. Games, PhD. The Chief Minister had members of the Peoples Democratic Movement (PDM) and the Progressive National Party (PNP) who supported him in this war, too. Some people in both parties still supported the drug cartels because they funded the PNP political party. The biggest secret JAGS had was that he knew the identities of all the men and women who worked to help the enemy. The Chief Minister's knowledge of his people was so great that he was able to use everyone in the battle to save his country, even while some continued to support the enemy. **That's a FACT.**

In this historical adventure story, the bad guys and gals are not named; even their descriptions have been changed. What they did is true fact, but it is not the purpose of this story to change history. Even some of the captures of the drug planes and pilots may not be in the correct order of events. Most of the Patriots are not named, and some may not even know of the important part they played in the Secret Islands Drug War or in the United States Space Program. **That's a FACT.**

The story is in Large Print (14 point) so the author can read the words that he has written, but sometimes not the complete paragraph. The Veterans Administration doctors have diagnosed Myasthenia Gravis (MG). It literally means "grave muscle weakness." It is a serious, potentially life threatening, neuromuscular, auto-immune disease which causes severe weakness in the voluntary muscles of the body. MG can affect a person's ability to see, speak, walk, smile, eat, and at its worst even to draw breath. It saps strength, erodes abilities and hope. It can halt a career, and even unravel the fabric of families. **That's a FACT.**

Helen M. Games, MBA, stands at the
sign welcoming tourists to
Grand Turk.

HOW IT BEGAN

My name is Montana. I'm a male, ninety-pound black Labrador Retriever trained as a Guide Dog with police experience, and my job is to be the Games Clan's Security Chief and companion to Helen. Sometimes her husband, Ben, is asked to check on a problem by someone he calls Harry. If it's serious or a mystery, then Helen and I join him. As a team, we remove the trouble or make it go away. We try to help people even though sometimes it isn't in a way they like or want.

The best time to nap in the Florida sun is during the morning before the pool deck heats up. This morning my pack mates are all sunbathing on the patio with me. Helen, my companion, has finished her chores and is telling Ben about my latest dream. He is making notes in his journal about our new assignment.

Smoky is in a chair with his front paws tucked under his chest pretending he is the Egyptian Sphinx or whatever cats think about when they are napping. Taffy, the yapping poodle, is walking around the swimming pool. She is getting on in years, and her eyesight is failing. I expect she will want me to guide her when she can no longer walk without falling into the water. I'll have to do it, since I'm the only one in the Games Clan who has graduated from Guide Dog School. For a six pound dog, she can be a pain in the tail. I really don't need her to stand and bark in my face just to tell me guests are at the front door.

The sun's rays are warm, and I can hardly keep my eyes open. It's quiet and Taffy isn't barking for once. There is only the beautiful voice of my companion telling Ben about my dreams. My new Teddy Bear that Santa brought me for Christmas is laying under my right paw. Then, quicker than a cat's spring, I'm back in my dream world at the time of the sinking of the drug ship, Carol "B", in the Turks & Caicos Islands, BWI.

The last thing I remember was Helen saying, "Ben, it looks like Montana is in another Italian Sogo." To me it's just a continuation of my dream about our battle to help Chief Minister James Alexander George Smith (JAGS) McCartney protect the Turks & Caicos Islands from the Columbian drug cartels.

As I lay dreaming by the swimming pool at our home in Apollo Beach, Florida, I was still on duty. Even asleep I keep one ear open. If Helen stops working and sits down to watch TV, Taffy will jump on her lap and I will have to get up to push her off. I have to watch Taffy and Smoky all the time. If I let my guard down for even a minute, those two will take advantage of my napping and get all of Helen's attention.

Suddenly Taffy sounded an alarm that woke me with a start. Someone was at the front door. I have to check to see who it is to make her stop barking. I don't bark, but I do woof at Helen when I need to go outside.

I do not fool around. If I need to give a warning, the hair on my back will stand up, and I'll growl deep down in my throat. To protect her, I get in front of my companion and move her out of danger. My message to any intruder is clear: Stay away. The best way to protect my companion is to move her to a safe area. Sometimes she will let me lead the way, and sometimes I have to push her, but there is no way I will let anything harm her.

I joined Helen as she opened the door. There were two US Army officers standing there. One had stars on his shirt collar, and the other one was wearing an eagle. Helen knew them and greeted them saying, "Welcome General Phillips, Colonel Case. Come in. I'll tell Ben you're here." Then she introduced me and invited everyone to walk out to the pool area where they could sit and drink iced tea. Ben joined us, and while they made small talk I lay down at Helen's feet and went back to sleep. I often do this so people will relax, but I always lay so they cannot reach Helen without going over me, and I'm listening to every word.

These men were friends of Ben's and had flown with him many times in the US Army. They asked questions about the Turks & Caicos Islands and offered suggestions for what could be done to stop the flow of drugs from there into the United States. The only problem was they all knew that fighting the drug cartels was a deadly political war, besides being a killing field which was political taboo to talk about with the African- and Mexican-Americans. Ben told them about how he believed this was an extension of the Vietnam War and was an attack on the Christian Churches of the American people. The only things standing directly in the way of this

Dark Force and the drug cartels were Chief Minister JAGS McCartney, and the Patriots of the Turks & Caicos Islands.

On the island of Grand Turk it's nice to know that you can go outside to go "busy-busy" and never encounter a temperature below 77° F or above 83° F all year round. The only thing I have to remember is that some time after midnight and before dawn's light breaks it usually rains. I don't like to pee in the rain, besides it's hard to get my companion Helen to walk with me in the rain at night. Most nights Fuujin, the Okinawa God of Wind, moves the rain showers over the white sandy beaches, causing the clouds to hide a sky full of sparkling stars.

It is a beautiful, peaceful land but there is a real danger lurking here. There are no fences, and the donkeys run in herds. Five donkeys are living in a field nearby, and many times I've heard them running at a full gallop through the yard at night. When going "busy-busy" I have to jump and run to get out of their way. It's not very dignified having to stop peeing and run to keep from being knocked over by a bunch of animals. I don't like donkeys, and whenever one is near I growl so everyone knows I'm serious.

As a member of the Games Clan, I travel all over the world helping solve mysteries and doing research for Ben's books. When people ask Ben who he works for, he tells them it is for God and Country. I'm not sure if they understand him, but our work is always an adventure even though it's sometimes dangerous. Ben keeps a journal for each assignment we work on. As chief security dog for the team, I recruit and organize the local dogs into an intelligence network that gathers information needed to solve the problem. My most important job, though, is showing Helen where the bathroom is and protecting her from danger.

In the story *Santa's Secret*, I helped Santa find the lost letters written by the children of the Turks & Caicos Islands. This adventure story is about how I organized the dogs on the Turks & Caicos Islands to help stop the Columbian drug cartels from making South Caicos into the drug capital of the Caribbean. The chapter titled "Historical Documents" will help the reader see that this was truly a special time where ordinary people became Patriots of the Turks & Caicos Islands. It is also part of the history of the Games Family Clan and how we helped JAGS McCartney protect the people of the islands against the Columbian drug cartels.

At the time of this story there were two political parties on the Islands: The People's Democratic Movement (PDM), headed by the First Elected Chief Minister of the islands, the Honorable JAGS McCartney; and the Royal Opposition party named the Progressive National Party (PNP), led by Norman Saunders. These men had the same goal, making their country economically strong so everyone had a job. They had the same goal, but came up with two different paths for their county to follow. JAGS, leader of the PDM, would give his life in the battle fighting the Columbian drug cartels, and Norman, leader of the PNP, would be elected as the 3rd Chief Minister of his country. Later he would be arrested in Miami and imprisoned for accepting a bribe. His government was also doing nothing to stop a wide-open narcotics smuggling business.

These were two men serving their country with two different methods. One of the islands, South Caicos, would become known as a Smuggler's Paradise. This island was where the Secret Islands' Drug War was started by those trying to protect their country.

The Turks & Caicos Islands were directly in the path of other nations' political agendas, and were also needed by the United States for its space program. Some nations attempted to take the islands away from the people by signing documents allowing the United Nations to bring in Vietnamese boat people. They did this knowing that within a few years, the Vietnamese would have enough votes to take control of the islands' government. Others tried to use the drug trade to control the islands, while the Communists, through the KGB, made plans to corrupt and influence the islands' leaders by placing specially trained female communist agents in contact with the government ministers. They were to use their sexual skills to influence votes and cause dissension. If that didn't work they were to cause accidents or assassinate those who got in their way.

The United Nations plan worked up to a point. Ben read the documents signed by the Turks & Caicos Islands' government ministers. This document said they agreed to allow five hundred Vietnamese boat people and their families to be flown into the islands. Ben noticed that there was nothing in the agreement about Vietnamese dogs or that the islands were a self-governing British Colony. In this plan, he total number of Vietnamese boat people and their families would be over 3000.

The first families were due to arrive by leased airline planes within the next thirty days. At this time the capital, Cockburn Town (Grand Turk), had a population of 3500 people and 162 dogs; Salt Cay, 400 people and 23 dogs; South Caicos, 1300 people and 51 dogs; Middle Caicos, 450 people and 18 dogs; Providenciales, 900 people and 43 dogs. With the number of Vietnamese boat people coming into the country, the shock to the islands' culture would be beyond belief. The island's government was promised $1000 US dollars per family plus an annual support fee of $500 dollars per year for each family over a 5 year period.

When Ben asked Governor Strong if he knew how many people were involved in each Vietnamese family, the governor told him that it didn't really matter because the planes would not be allowed to land; and they never did.

Under the Communist's diabolical secret plan, the KGB proposed that five baby girls be found and trained to be undercover secret agents with a license to kill. When these agents were fully trained and ready, they would be used to further the interests of the Communists all over the world. The babies were kidnapped directly from hospitals, but had to meet specific specifications. They were beautiful baby girls who grew up to be stunning, deadly women. All the children were kept in an orphanage located deep within Russia. Funding records and knowledge of their training was secret from everyone except Stalin and the KGB people in control of the operation.

The plan was approved one snowy November day in 1960. By the spring of 1961, all the babies were in the custody of the KGB. No one wanted to believe such a plan was a fact, but rumors with bits and pieces of evidence surfaced from time to time. The CIA and MI-6 classified the rumors as top secret for the eyes of the American President or British Prime Minister only.

My dog cohort/agents came upon evidence of the communist plot's existence from information uncovered during intelligence surveillance while looking for drug shipments. We knew someone with the backing of a secret intelligence organization was working against the Turks & Caicos Islands' government, but we didn't know who. Ben thought it could be one of these special KGB agents helping the Communist Cuban government.

As Chief Security Officer, I recruited all the dogs in the islands into one large intelligence-gathering organization. My organization was so good that it was never compromised. I was able to learn top-secret information from the most closely guarded places. The President of the United States unknowingly provided information that confirmed our information about one of these women. He was scratching his Beagle hound's ear one day while discussing the KGB special agents with the Prime Minister of Britain in the Rose Garden of the White House. His dog was one of my cohort/agents, and he passed the information along by peeing on the fence next to where the public walks on Pennsylvania Avenue. Another of my agents read the message and it was passed on in a similar manner until it arrived in Grand Turk on an Air Florida plane's tire. I received the message three days after the conversation took place.

The only problem in my organization was that I was never able to figure out how to use female dogs to send information on airplane tires. The ladies made fine agents, but I was never able to teach them how to pee on an airliner's tires so they could send their messages directly to me.

On Grand Turk my cohort/agents would check the tires of all the planes after they landed. They would read any messages they found, then relay them to me at our home on Airport Road in Cockburn Town. They even checked for messages coming from other countries on the private planes that landed. This worked on Grand Turk but not on the other islands. My network was big, and there were so many dogs visiting our front yard that no grass would grow. Helen kept yelling at my agents, "Don't pee on the grass." She didn't need to bother after the first week, though, because there wasn't any grass left.

At this time, John Houseman of Grand Turk was telling stories about the history of the islands and their people to tourists at the Turks Head Inn and at the Hotel Kittina. He had retired from England's secret service after WW-II, and wrote stores about the ashes of the Austro-Hungarian Empire. One of his novels was about a baby girl from Count Czernin's family who was kidnapped in Hungary. Since the Count and his wife now lived on Pirate Cay, this was of interest to Ben because the Count's daughter was beautiful and appeared to be the right age to be one of the KGB's special agents.

We were trying hard to locate all the men and women working against the islands' government. Ben said if we could find and identify these people we might learn what they were going to try next. His plan was to hit them hard before they attacked us.

I have used this type of counter intelligence myself, and it works. One time I was with Helen close behind a young dog who was being trained to become a guide dog. He wasn't paying attention to his trainer and had been making eyes at Helen. I just bit him hard on his rump. He screamed and cried telling everyone he had been bitten. I just pretended nothing had happened. That trainer scolded all the dogs in the room but me. I just stood there looking like butter wouldn't melt in my mouth with Helen holding my harness. That pup stopped making eyes at my companion and never came near us again.

***

At one of our Clan's meetings Ben told us that we shouldn't expect the people to treat us any different than they treated each other. I personally think he is wrong, because sometimes when we visited the airport terminal building, the American flag would be laying on the ground where it fell after someone cut the lanyard holding it up. Governor Strong once told Ben that he could see the flagpoles from his office by using a ship's eyeglass, and that he could tell when the people were unhappy with the United States or him by what happened to the flags.

There were three flagpoles in front of the terminal building, one flew the British Union Jack, one the Stars and Strips, and in the center was the Turk & Caicos Islands flag. As long as we lived on Grand Turk, the American flag was flown at the airport. The only times it wasn't waving in the breeze were on the days when someone was unhappy about what Ben had done.

This was also true with Governor Strong. Ben seems to think that everyone likes what he is doing, and that they all want to help stop the Columbian drug cartels. I'm not so sure, because there are many days when our flag is down until Helen puts it back up.

Some days just the British Flag is down and once all the flags were down, and the Cuban flag was flying in place of the Turks & Caicos Islands flag. That was one time I saw Ben get really mad. He had a baggage handler lower the Cuban flag. No aircraft was allowed to load passengers or take off until the Turks & Caicos Flag was raised. The other flags were placed in their storage containers. The Cuban flag was sent to the governor's office.

It was a strange sight to see the bare flagpoles in front of the terminal building. Then Ben had a notice placed in the terminal building notifying all passengers that Air Florida Airline planes would not be arriving that day. Everyone got excited and people from town started coming to the airport to see what was wrong. No one seemed to remember that it was Tuesday and Air Florida had no flights scheduled on Tuesday.

Ben had told us many times that there are no secrets in the Turks & Caicos Islands. One of the reasons for this was the Confidential Relationship Ordinance Act of 1979. It imposes complete secrecy and confidentiality on the part of anyone in possession of confidential information howsoever obtained and provides severe legal sanctions for breach of express or implied conditions of professional or commercial confidence. This makes many visitors believe that all business transactions are secret. Actually the people understand the law, and to avoid getting into trouble they make sure nothing is ever confidential or secret.

One time the Minister of Tourism and Development, Liam Maguire, wrote a bad check for a thousand dollars and cashed it at the TCNA ticket sales office. He then invoked the law stating that this was a confidential matter, and the country's attorney general agreed. Ben was the manager of TCNA, so he published all the checks received by the airline. They were then placed on a public bulletin board in the airport terminal with a notice that checks written to the airline were part of the public record. The check from Liam Maguire was there too, stamped by the bank as "returned, no funds." Ben then gave a list of names to the airline ticket agents of those individuals who had to pay in cash. Maguire and family were on the cash-only list.

***

Ben held a meeting with the entire Clan on Grand Turk after the sinking of the drug ship Carol "B". During the meeting he told us that we would never fight unless it was to win. He must have forgotten that I don't have hands when he told us to never hit someone with our fists if a club was handy, and never leave a live enemy behind us. He explained about the need to protect the people who help us, and that we should never trust a jackass to help in case of trouble. I agreed with him completely. Even if I have to bite them, I'll never trust those donkeys.

I was reading messages near our back porch when I heard the donkeys coming again. They were at a full gallop and I had to jump up on the porch to get out of their way. There were four mares, and a stallion was nipping at their tails. They passed so close that two of the mares actually touched the wooden rail I was standing behind. I growled, but didn't bark since it would be like barking into the wind. The only thing more dangerous than this scenario is when you see a mare with her new colt. The baby is friendly and cute, but mama isn't. She won't give any warning before kicking you with both hind legs at the same time. She can even kick sideways with both feet off the ground. If she connects, something breaks. Beware, it isn't only the back end that's dangerous; donkeys can bite, too.

This morning on the way from the airport to our house, Ben stopped in across the street from the airline's main office to tell Stanley E. Williams, Commissioner of Police, about the sinking of the drug ship Carol "B". Ben had just arrived from South Caicos. As he entered the police headquarters, the Commissioner saw him and called out, "Ben, come on in. I just heard from

South Caicos that you were on your way home. It was on an unsecured phone line, and Police Inspector Lightburn said it was a good flight. Sit and tell me everything."

My cohort/agent who was on duty at police headquarters was pretending to scratch and catch a flea near his tail as he sat in the Police Commissioner's office. No one pays any attention to a dog working on an itch, so he heard everything.

Ben was sitting in a chair across from the Police Commissioner and starting to tell what had happened in the South Caicos Fishing Banks. Suddenly a Scotland Yard detective came rushing into the office saying, "Commissioner, the drug boat Scotland Yard's been tracking is on its way to South Caicos." Then he saw Ben sitting in the chair and stopped.

"It's okay, the commissioner told him, "Ben and I are just visiting."

"I've just received word from Scotland Yard that the ship finished loading and sailed at 0100 hours for South Caicos," he continued, acting very nervous. He was trying to talk so Ben wouldn't know what he was talking about.

Ben is bad about taking advantage of someone who thinks they know more than him, and nonchalantly said, "If you're talking about the Carol "B", I was just reporting to Commissioner Williams that his plan worked. I sank her at daylight.".

The Commissioner was practically beaming as he told the Scotland Yard detective he should notify his supervisor that the problem was solved.

After they were alone he relaxed back in his chair and asked Ben to finish telling him everything. When Ben was finished, he said, "I'll brief Governor Strong that the threat to South Caicos from the Carol "B" is gone, but I think we'll give Scotland Yard credit for getting us the information about the drug shipment on the Carol "B". I'll also brief JAGS on how everyone worked to help sink the ship. I think we'd better forget about just how it was done. It's funny how everyone gets nervous when we talk."

***

One evening I heard Ben tell Helen that this island situation was almost as bad as when we were flying missions in Vietnam. Helen answered, "It is, except we don't have to worry about a mortar attack at night and we can go to our home in Florida for a few day's rest whenever we need a break from the tension. I agree, though, this war is almost as deadly as it was in Vietnam, and the drug cartel is a lot like the North Vietnamese or maybe worse."

As I lay napping, Helen added that we were just about out of drinking water and needed groceries. She bought bottled water in Miami and brought it here for us to drink so we wouldn't get sick. There were no wells or rivers in the Turks & Caicos Islands, only cisterns holding rainwater. I heard Ben tell her that we would catch a ride on the USAF shuttle flight tomorrow afternoon and spend a few days in Florida so she could shop.

The plan was to spend a week at our home in Apollo Beach, Florida, resting and purchasing supplies for our home on Grand Turk. I don't know why Ben needed a break, since I do most of the work. It wasn't necessary for him to be with us, because I could take Helen shopping and Bud was there to carry the grocery bags into the house.

***

We'd been home for three days, and I was napping beside the pool listening to Ben and Helen tell Colonel Case and General Phillips about what we were doing in the islands. The phone rang, and Helen went to answer it. She called out, "It's the Honorable JAGS McCartney. He says you should see him before you attend the governor's meeting on Monday. He seems worried, even though I told him we would be back Thursday afternoon. He wants to speak to you."

After Ben finished talking on the phone to JAGS, he came back out to the pool deck where General Phillips and Colonel Case were drinking iced tea with Helen. "That was a strange call," he told them. "The Chief Minister wants me to meet with Lewis Astwood, Minister of Public Works, on Friday. He said he couldn't tell me more right now, and that Lewis would explain everything when I get to Grand Turk," Ben added, acting like he was already getting ready to leave.

"Art and Verse have just arrived. You can't leave now," Helen said.

"Don't worry about us," Art said. "It sounds important. We can visit some other time."

I went inside with Helen while she made phone calls to Air Florida Airlines to arrange for Ben's ticket. After the reservations were made, we went back out to the patio where Ben was telling his friends about how we'd become the owners of a new housing subdivision on Grand Turk during a vacation last year.

"You'll leave from Tampa on Delta tomorrow at noon and transfer to Air Florida in Miami," Helen told Ben.

Drifting back into my dream world, I remembered how we first got drafted into joining JAGS in his fight to stop the drug lords from taking control of the national airline. Just before I closed my eyes, I heard Ben call out to Helen, "I'll phone you when I find out what their problem is and how we can help."

I really don't worry about Ben when he is away. This wasn't the first time he'd gone ahead to research a story or investigate a mystery. If it's interesting or there's something we can do to help, he'll phone and Helen will pack our bags so we can join him. I'll watch to be sure she doesn't forget my Teddy Bear. Some people laugh when they see a big dog like me carrying a Teddy Bear when we are traveling, but it makes a soft pillow for my head at night.

We had to wait three days before Ben called, and then all he would tell us was that we were to join him on Grand Turk. He also told us we now had a three bedroom house and our own airplane. Helen asked him how much that was going to cost us, and I heard him laugh when he told her that the Turks & Caicos Islands' government was picking up the tab and had even agreed to pay all of our expenses.

She tried to get him to tell us how much dog food to bring and what clothing to pack. He wouldn't even tell us the day we should travel. I remember his instructions, because they were a little unusual. We were to show our papers and passports at the ticket desk of Air Florida when we wanted to leave for Grand Turk. We didn't need to get advance reservations because there would be seats reserved on every flight until we actually used them.

Anyone who wanted to know that we were returning to the Turks & Caicos Islands could find out, but not even the airline could tell them when. In fact, only Helen and I would know. Our Ben has always said the only way to keep a secret was not to have one.

Helen made the usual arrangements for Ben Jr. (Bud) and Jon to pick up the mail and keep the house open. Jon would take us to the Tampa Airport when we were ready to leave. They both knew we were leaving, but not what day. They didn't get that information until an hour before we needed a ride to the airport. Whatever the problem in the islands was, it must be serious or dangerous. We've followed Ben to some strange places, but this time he didn't even want to know when we would be traveling. He told us later that he didn't want to know in advance because it could've caused him to change his schedule or do something different that could've endangered us.

Ben didn't have to worry, because I check all the messages my cohorts leave for me in Apollo Beach, Florida, two or three times a day. They also knew we were leaving, and I didn't tell them when either. Security is my middle name, and in this situation only Helen knew the date.

Two weeks went by before she phoned Jon and told him to pick us up. Another member of our team, Bud, was told to prepare for a trip to the islands if we needed him. Then she got my working harness ready and said, "Let's go."

When we got to the check-in counter at the airport, she asked for the tickets to Miami. They turned out to be one-way first class tickets all the way to Grand Turk, BWI. I was to travel for free and sit in the seat beside her. That's the *only* way to travel. Being a working Guide Dog and a private investigator does have its advantages.

Everyone knows that dogs are color blind, even me — a specially trained dog with telepathic ability. My nose is very good, though. With it, messages from other dogs are easy to read. Plus, using mental telepathy helps with understanding what Helen is seeing and feeling. (When I tell about colors, I am really telling you what she is seeing.) Sometimes she pretends she doesn't understand my messages, but I know she can if she tries hard enough.

Grand Turk is an island located an hour and thirty minutes from Miami by jet airliner. It's an island a mile and a half wide and six miles long. When we arrived, Ben was waiting. He told us that he had met every incoming flight since his phone call asking us to come. I wagged my tail acknowledging him, but was more interested in finding a bush were I could start checking on messages my local cohort/agent dogs may have left. I still didn't know the mystery that we had to solve, but I know my job. We would need all the information I could get. Reading other peoples' mail is a good place to start.

That evening Ben briefed us on what the Chief Minster was asking us to do and why it was so dangerous. He started by telling us how he'd waited three days to talk with the Minister of Labor, Lewis Astwood. He'd finally given up and decided they must've changed their minds about needing our help. That very day, Lewis came to Hotel Kittina where Ben was eating lunch. He brought D.H. (Curly) Walters with him. They stopped by Ben's table and visited for a moment. After the introductions were made, Walters asked Ben to meet him in the bar at 1800-hours. Lewis said he couldn't join them, but asked Ben to let him know what they decided.

Who Curly Walters was and what he had to do with the Turks & Caicos Islands' government was a mystery. No one in the hotel knew anything about him. All they could tell Ben was that he'd arrived on Grand Turk five days before; which was the day JAGS had phoned asking for our help. He'd spent every day since then in meetings with Governor Strong and various government ministers.

"Who was he? What is their problem, and how can we help?" Helen asked.

I'd already read messages from most of the island's dogs and knew that a lot of drugs were being moved through here to the United States. The Air Florida plane's luggage ramp reeked with the smell of the stuff, and even the luggage cart smelled sweet from contact with it. The customs area, where all the luggage was stored before loading it onto the airline, smelled like a drug storeroom. The smell as so strong that even with my great nose I couldn't tell exactly which suitcases contained drugs.

Ben likes to drag out a story, but Helen would have none of that. She wants the bottom line up front. She always tells him, "Start with why we are here, and then you can fill me in." My companion is like that. Me, I just lay down, listen, and sometimes think about that cute dog I saw peeing in the sand by the front gate.

Ben said that he'd learned Curly Walters was the managing director of the aircraft sales division of British Caledonian Airlines. They had a contract with the Turks & Caicos Islands' government to furnish consulting services and assist them in operating TCNA.

TCNA was on the verge of bankruptcy, and one of Columbia's largest drug cartels was trying to get control of its planes to move drugs over its routes and into the United States. The Turks & Caicos Islands' government, the British government, and the United States government were trying to stop the drug lords by police action. "They want to save the airline without using their military forces to keep the drug war as a local police action. That's why we've been asked to help," Ben concluded.

Ben had been back on Grand Turk for two weeks and he was smiling as he told the story, so we knew he'd already started making things happen. He said that after talking with Curly, they'd decided that Ben would have to be in control of the airline and would take charge by 0800-hours the following morning. It had to take place before the drug cartel had time to organize an attack plan to stop him.

Curly, all the government ministers, and Ben met at 2200-hours in the government chambers on Front Street. JAGS, the Chief Minister, chaired the meeting but didn't make a presentation, instead he had Curly introduce Ben. "JAGS asked for our help, but he obviously didn't want anyone knowing that we worked for him," Ben told Helen.

Curly Walters had flown over from England to interview Ben, but neither he nor anyone at British Caledonia Airlines guessed that we were already working for the Chief Minister. The questions and speeches went on until 0200-hours. JAGS had sent for all the pilots and Lionel Saunders, the present TCNA General Manager, and asked them to wait in the visitor's room just off the meeting hall.

Ben said every time he thought they were ready to vote, Liam Maguire, Minister of Development, would bring up another question. He finally asked if Ben was prejudiced against blacks like most Americans. Ben said this question caught him by surprise, and he just sat there for a minute trying to think of how to answer.

Finally, the Chief Minister spoke up and said, "I'm not prejudiced against whites. Do I hear a motion for a vote?" A second to the motion came immediately after.

Ben said Liam was so surprised that he opened his mouth but didn't have time to say anything before the vote was taken. The Chief Minister instructed the secretary to record the vote as unanimous for Ben to be a member of the Board of Directors of TCNA and to act as General manager. Ben said he just looked at Liam the whole time he said this.

After that, JAGS shook Ben's hand and asked him in a low voice when he would take control. Ben told him he would be in the TCNA comptroller's office at 0800-hours. JAGS just nodded and called for the guard to bring the visitors into the room. Ben talked with the pilots for a few minutes, and then told Lionel that he would meet with him at 0900-hours. At this point, none of them knew Ben was a pilot. By 0230-hours it was all over.

I'll bet no one expected to see me when I arrived with Helen a few weeks later. After the meeting, Ben returned to the Kittina hotel to phone Helen and ask everyone to join him. Helen has a MBA degree in business, and her job would be to help teach the airline controller how to organize the accounting office to help keep the airline out of bankruptcy. She would also notify the World Bank that the Turks & Caicos National Airline was now under Ben's control.

Ben's first job was to stop drugs from being transported by the airline and at the same time support the Commissioner of Police, Stanley E. Williams, in capturing drug planes. My job, as always, was to manage the clan's security and set up an intelligence gathering network to obtain information that would help track the movement of drugs as well as the bad guys.

***

The first test of the airline under Ben's direction had happened just before Helen and I arrived. Ben had fired the Brazilian Chief Pilot of the airline and a pilot from Haiti. They were not charged with moving drugs, but were forced to leave the country because they lost their employment. He also made a requirement that all luggage and freight be inspected at the plane prior to its being loaded. This is when the test came.

Earl "Super C" Ingram, head of the baggage handlers on Grand Turk, organized and led the first strike against the airline in island history. The strike caused everything in the country to shut down, so the government ministers met as a committee to decide the airline's future. Once again they voted to support Ben, and the airline had a chance to survive.

The strike did have one positive affect for the employees, Ben and "Super C" realized they were both working to help the people of the Turks & Caicos Islands. They decided that together they could do more for the islands than they could fighting each other.

The day after the strike ended, Ben asked "Super C" to meet him in the airline's main office on the road next to Prospere's Tailor Shop. Ben had never met with him before, so when he walked in "Super C" expected to be fired or at the least reprimanded. He was in for a surprise, though. Ben stood up behind the desk where he'd been sitting, then walked across the office to meet "Super C" at the door. "The airline has an opening for a personnel officer," Ben told him. "We need someone who knows the area and is dedicated in his desire to help all TCNA employees. I watched you organize them in the strike, and I think you can fill the position. Would you like to join me?" Ben asked as he shook the surprised man's hand.

"You won, and the strike failed," "Super C" said sullenly.

"Not so," Ben said. "We both won. All the employees got their back pay, and the men who controlled the drug traffic on TCNA are being deported.

"If you accept the position, your first job will be to put the deaf-mute baggage handler at the airport on Grand Turk in charge of all baggage handling," Ben told him

"When do I start?" he asked.

"You've started. I've been sitting at your desk waiting for you," Ben said and offered him the chair. He smiled and told "Super C" that he was going to the hangar to visit with Marsh Greene, chief aircraft engineer, and Keith Malcolm, his assistant.

***

Things move fast when Ben is getting his teeth into a problem. In less than two weeks he had almost stopped the shipping of drugs on TCNA aircraft. He decided it would be hard for the drug people to make a deal with the baggage handlers when the man in charge couldn't hear or speak and had just been given a better paying job than he'd ever held before. Plus, the drug cartel couldn't put their people in position to keep the drugs flowing because the new personnel director was a friend of the Chief Minister and had been the head of security for the PDM before starting to work for the airline.

Now that Helen and I were with Ben, our team was almost ready to go on the offensive. First, Helen had to send for Bud and get him working to secure a direct supply line for the airline. He would travel from Grand Turk to Tampa or Miami where equipment and supplies were purchased for TCNA. Helen would watch the money trail while Bud would oversee and inspect the movement of all supply shipments. "Super C" and Lionel Saunders would watch over the employees and schedule the routes to the islands serviced by the airline. Now Ben could do the job the Chief Minister had really asked him to do.

When Curly Walters briefed him about the problem of drugs being hauled on TCNA aircraft, Ben quickly realized that Curly thought he was a banker and businessman who was applying for the job of General Manager. Curly had no idea that JAGS had actually *sent* for Ben.

We suspected that no one knew Ben's background in aviation or that he was an airline and military senior pilot. We also believed that no one would guess that Helen was also a licensed twin-engine pilot and that I had police training. We agreed that it was best if we kept this information to ourselves. This way, if we had to move to get out of danger no one would be watching the airline's aircraft. Ben had even made arrangements so we could fly to Puerto Plata in the Dominican Republic if we had to leave in a hurry. Puerto Plata is 110 miles south of Grand Turk, and even a Cessna-172 could make the trip.

There is also a US Air Force down-range missile and spacecraft tracking station on the south end of Grand Turk, but no security police guard it. On the days that Air Florida didn't fly into Grand Turk from Miami, the USAF had a scheduled military transport flight stopping at all the Caribbean USAF bases. Ben used the military transport planes to move around the Caribbean to avoid alerting the bad guys during our battle with the drug cartels. We were really on our own, except for the Turks & Caicos Islands' police, and the enemy outgunned them. The police were willing and able, but didn't have the firepower to fight a pitched battle.

Bud was due to arrive the following week, and I'd already visited all seven of the active airstrips with Ben and Helen. At each stop, I had recruited the dogs to watch and leave messages telling me when drugs were being moved or stored. It was not hard to organize this network, since I have never met a dog who didn't want to help his or her companion. All I had to do was assure them that I could tell Helen any information they passed along and she would tell Ben.

I've heard people talk about Ben, saying he must be a great dog lover because all dogs wag their tails when they see him and are excited as they greet him. Actually, they just want to pee on his leg so I will get their message when he returns home. Ben has told me many times that I have to find some other means of communication because he always has to watch out for dogs who try to pee on him, and it was making people talk.

TCNA airline uses twin-engine Islander aircraft with fixed landing gear. All I had to do was restrict my recruiting to male dogs. They would leave their messages on the tires of the planes. It worked perfectly because planes were landing at each airport in the country every two hours, and there were dogs waiting to check each wheel when the planes returned to Grand Turk. The furthest airport from Grand Turk was at Providenciales (Provo) only an hour away, and the shortest flight was a six-minute hop to Salt Cay; only the police had faster communications.

***

My father , Vermont, was the top breeder dog at Southeastern Guide Dog School where I was trained as a Guide Dog. All working guide dogs are neutered so they will not be distracted while taking care of their companions. My police training came while I was assigned to a blind undercover drug detective. Now I'm a private investigator working as a service dog. I am very big, black, and handsome. The ladies fall in love at first sight and I like the attention, but Ben is not too happy about it.

One day a lady I'd never met saw Ben while he was visiting Pine Cay and peed on his shoe. When he returned to Grand Turk, he told me a lady had sent a message and it might be important. After reading it, I didn't know how to tell him that it was actually a love letter. I told Helen the letter was garbled, and I couldn't understand the message. Actually, I would like to meet that young lady because the message told about all the things she was going to do for me when we met.

***

My work as part of the team is top-secret, but still two of my cohort/agents were killed during the first month we were on Grand Turk. Losing an agent is bad, but twice as bad when they are dogs who are working to protect the people they love.

One night some men who were loading marijuana into one of TCNA's planes caught my agents. They were taken to a field south of the airport and tortured before they were killed. When Bud arrived, Ben had him investigate and take the evidence to the Commissioner of Police who pressed charges at Ben's request. No one took the case seriously, but two men were convicted and fined five dollars each. Ben couldn't tell the Commissioner they were part of the drug cartel because it would've given our source of information away.

"We now know two of our enemies. With a $5 fine and the threat of having to appear in court, the drug pushers will just throw rocks at your agents in the future," Ben told me. "They will never know that they've been identified as workers for the drug cartel. Tell your agents to run and stay out of reach of anyone loading or unloading drugs. There is a great danger here and it's only going to get worse."

We had only lived in Cockburn Town, the capital of the Turks & Caicos Islands, a few weeks when the drug cartel tried a new tactic against the crackdown on moving marijuana through the islands on its way to Florida. I received information from the dogs on South Caicos that the airport expected a large plane full of marijuana to arrive in three days. It was to be flown into South Caicos from Columbia in a twin-engine Convair.

The information came from many different dogs living on South Caicos. The messages all told about the marijuana and cocaine that would be sold to drug dealers visiting the airport. It would be loaded directly into the drug dealers' planes from the cartel's Convair. The drugs would arrive at noon, sales would be made, transfers completed, and the drug dealers' planes would take off for different points in the US. They were all scheduled to arrive after nightfall. The South Caicos airport was to become a drug dealers' flea market, and the cartel would no longer need TCNA planes.

That night Helen and Ben were sitting on the porch under

a sky full of stars that were so bright it seemed like you could reach up and touch them. Helen looked up and said, "Queen Mab couldn't have asked for anything more." I wagged my tail twice just to let her know I agreed, even though I wondered who Queen Mab was.

This photograph shows the white sand beaches
of Grand Turk and below is a map of the islands.

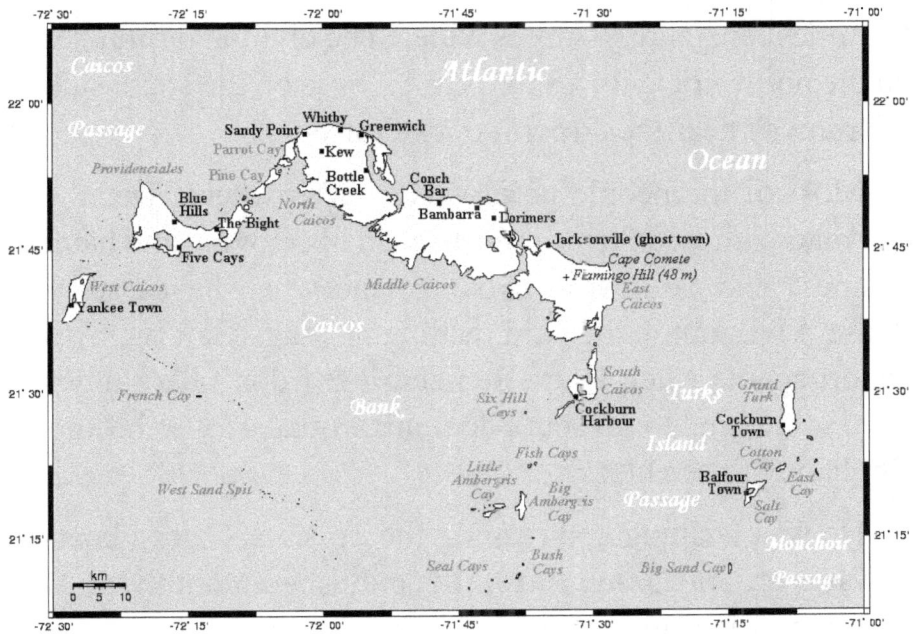

DEATH OF A PATRIOT

The day after finding out about the cartel's latest plan, Ben attended the morning pilots' briefing at the hangar. Afterwards, he stopped to visit Stanley Williams at Police Headquarters. When Ben left the Police Commissioner's office, he walked towards the TCNA office on Airport Road. His trek took him right by Cockburn Town's only gas station, which was busy with two cars. At 0800-hours, these were the only cars around because they were also used as taxicabs.

No one was in a hurry this morning because TCNA flights to the other islands had already left at 0700-hours, and the regular incoming flights would not start arriving until 0900-hours.

The airport's runway runs east to west and was 5000 feet long. It's located a mile south of town. (Grand Turk is an island 6½ miles long and 1½ miles wide.) The civilian terminal was on the north side with a small USAF base on the south side of the runway near the airport control tower.

Most of the people here walked everywhere. There was one man with a donkey cart he used in his moving and hauling business and he always spoke to me when he passed our house. I was out in the yard reading messages left by my dog cohort/agents when I saw Ben coming. I don't bark unless I have something to say, but I do jump around a lot so he knows I'm happy to see him.

He was walking and reading the Turks & Caicos Islands' newspaper, *The Green Flash*. It's published monthly by Don Cay Associates and reports many politically inspired stories.

Ben told Helen that the paper never had stories about the Islands' Drug War, but you could guess at what was going to affect TCNA's operations by the paper's reports on the actions of the country's two political parties. The PDM (People's Democratic Movement), headed by Chief Minister JAGS McCartney, was the majority political party in 1980, and the PNP (Progressive National Party), headed by Norman Saunders, was the Royal Opposition party.

The Turks & Caicos Islands' National Airline (TCNA) was a major employer in the islands, and was the only transportation between islands for most of the people. There were a few local pilots who were licensed by TCNA to provide charter flights, but none flew scheduled routes. Under Ben's leadership the airline was slowly growing and had accumulated more working capital in Barclay's Bank on Grand Turk than the local government. This put TCNA on the front line for most of the political arguments in the parliamentary arena.

Sometimes it wasn't what the paper reported, but what it didn't that interested Ben. The paper had never reported on the secret drug war that JAGS was fighting and never said anything about the sinking of a drug ship in the Caicos Fishing Banks. The country was engaged in a life and death struggle in a war that no one in the islands talked about or wrote about. The newspapers in the United States carried horror stories about the fighting and people dying in the Islands' drug war, but no one called it a war except JAGS, the Chief Minister. Even the newspapers in the United States and Great Britain referred to the war as a "police action."

(I've heard Helen tell Ben that it was a lot like the Korean Police Action only much smaller. Even some of the Turks & Caicos Islands' government ministers and businessmen were trying to make money from the Columbian drug cartels that were smuggling drugs into the United States through the islands.)

Castro's Cuban government, representing the Communists who wanted Russia to become the first to establish a base on the moon, and the Columbian drug cartels were the enemies in this war. No one even considered that it could be the Chinese astronauts who would release the China dragon on the moon.

Supporting the Turks & Caicos Islands' people were the United States government, even though it wouldn't admit it was involved in fighting a war, and the British government, that wanted the problem to be solved as a police action so the United Nations wouldn't become involved. There were also many patriots of the Turks & Caicos Islands in the fight; men and women who placed their country first.

All the dogs of the islands were truly Turks & Caicos Islands' patriots, too, and worked as cohort/intelligence agents in my organization. Leading the fight in this minefield of intrigue was James Alexander George Smith (JAGS) McCartney, who's skill and expertise kept the other government ministers distracted so Ben could carry out his assignments.

Once, when the British Governor and Mrs. Strong were having dinner at our home, the Governor said that he didn't know how Ben was able to get both political parties to agree on laws to intercept smugglers. He ended up saying, "Whatever you're doing, keep it up." Then he added, "The British Foreign Office has prepared a profile on the members of the Islands' Parliament who always vote against any laws putting restrictions on smuggling, currency controls, and banking. There is one minister on the list that may interest you. My instructions are to let you read the files, but only in my office. I can give you thirty minutes tomorrow at 1130-hours."

"I'll be there," Ben told him.

The next day, the governor's dog reported that Ben showed up exactly at the appointed time. The Governor met Ben at his office door, and after shaking hands, asked him to sit on the davenport facing a coffee table and his desk. After Ben had been seated, the governor placed a file folder on the coffee table and a clock facing Ben. "I have a luncheon meeting with the man named in the file and the Chief Minister (Premier) at 1230-hours. Every afternoon at 1600-hours, I run on the sandy beach in front of Government House. If you have any questions about the file you can join me," the Governor said. At the same time, he held up one finger and tapped his lips.

Ben just nodded. My cohort/agent reported that the governor's local staff all received gifts from people who wanted information, but no one knew about the Governor's dog who reported directly to me. In fact my agent reported that he went running on the beach with the governor every afternoon, and it was fun. Right then and there I knew that somehow I'd go with Ben that afternoon. After all, it's my duty as the Clan's Security Chief and Alpha dog.

Ben said the British Foreign Office report must've been prepared by MI-6 or the US CIA and was about the personal life of TCNA Chairman of the Board, Liam Maguire. He was also the Minister of Tourism and Development and the Representative for South Caicos. The report included things like copies of his bank accounts, his British Army military record, his voting record in the parliament of the Turks & Caicos Islands, his trips to Cuba, his love life, his marriage, and even his family problems. At the end there was a summary by a psychiatrist telling the reader about what to expect from any confrontation with this man.

That evening when Ben had finished telling us about the report he exclaimed, "The man is a coward!"

"I wonder what they have written about us?" Helen mused. I just rolled over on my back to get more comfortable and wagged my tail so they would know I was still listening. I agreed with Ben; if I raised my hackles and growled I bet Liam would run.

That very afternoon, Ben asked me to go for a run on the beach. He put on swimming trunks before asking if I wanted to go. There was no way I was going to miss this outing, but I had to check with Helen first. She even had to push me out the door so I would know it was all right. I think all guide dogs make their companions push them out of the house when they go off to play with someone else, just so they will feel that it's really their companion's idea.

I just wore my collar, so I was ready for the water. The Governor House beach was a mile from our house, and I checked for messages from my agents as we walked along. John, the governor, was already walking along the beach with his dog when we got there. I ran ahead and greeted my cohort/agent. We ran out and jumped into the crystal clear water together. It was sea water, and we could see the white sandy bottom and fish swimming below us. My agent kept diving, trying to catch a fish. Not me, the water was too salty for my taste, besides he never caught one anyway.

I was too busy to listen to what the governor and Ben were talking about. When we got home Ben told Helen everything, and it wasn't much. The Governor had told Ben the British Foreign Office had made arrangements for a British Frigate of the Royal Navy to pay a courtesy visit to Grand Turk. It was not a scheduled visit, but the Captain had been instructed to anchor off Cockburn Town and allow a few visitors to come aboard. Ben and the Commissioner of Police were invited to have lunch with him and his officers when the ship arrived in the area.

Ben said he'd asked if the Royal Marines would join the police force for raids against the drug cartel. The governor had told him that they couldn't interfere with a civil police action, but would furnish transport by launch or helicopter and stop any vessels at sea if the Police Commissioner asked them.

Ben said he had also asked about the times when they're visiting another island country, and the governor told him that the US Coast Guard was also going to visit South Caicos to check on the Loran "C" station and would be on East Caicos every week or two. He also said there should be a warship within 24 hours' distance to answer an emergency calls.

***

When Parliament was in session, Governor Strong acted as its chairman, even though he had no vote in case of a tie. With all the information furnished to his office by the British Foreign Office, Scotland Yard, and MI-6, he still hadn't guessed that JAGS had people in both political parties helping him fight to save the islands from the drug lords.

All the dogs in the Turks & Caicos Islands were also helping by reporting all smuggling operations they found. No one paid any attention to them, so they watched everything. They were everywhere gathering information and passing it on to me. Sometimes Helen pretended that she didn't understand what I was telling her. When she made a mistake in what she was telling Ben I'd have to sit and stare into her eyes, sending my message until she understood.

Sometimes, too, she complained that I wanted to go outside to read messages when it was raining or late at night. Another problem we had was how to pass the information my cohort/agents discovered to JAGS or the Commissioner of Police without telling them where it came from.

When God put these islands in just this place it was for his children who would someday need them. Now it was His people's turn to save the islands from those who would destroy them for drug money. My intelligence network was the best in the world, bar-none. My cohort/agents were loyal and dedicated to serving the people of the islands. The only problem I had was finding time to read all the messages and then finding enough pee to answer them.

***

Today was one of those lazy days with the temperature around 80 degrees and little wind. Air Florida had no scheduled flights today, so the only transportation between the islands was TCNA. Since Ben's attack on the Carol "B" this morning and its sinking, we weren't worried about the Columbian Drug Cartels trying to move drugs on any TCNA planes today.

It was turning out to be a beautiful day. Ben had returned from flying on the front lines early this morning, and Helen told me we were going to take the rest of the day off. We had lunch on the beach and watched the people coming from

Salt Cay to the pier on Front Street of Grand Turk to do their weekly shopping in Cockburn Town.

People came over to shop once a week courtesy of the owner of a large flat bottom barge. He would pull it, loaded with women shoppers and kids, from the Salt Cay to Grand Turk when the sea was calm. Since I had established intelligence agents on Salt Cay, there would also be one or two dogs on the barge. It was a way for me to get firsthand information about what was happening on the island and then pass it on to Helen.

Tonight we would have a meeting to plan how we could give the information to Stanley Williams, Commissioner of Police, so he could take action to protect the people from the drug cartels. (I'll bet he doesn't know that I'm the one doing most of the work.)

As the Games Clan's security chief and guide dog, I am always on duty, but I still enjoy meeting other dogs in person. It's also fun to run along the beach, but I never go far because I have to watch to be sure a wave doesn't try and get Helen. The little kids sometimes ask to pet me, and I give them a kiss when they do, but the adults never get too close. They know I'm a working dog and never crowd me. Even if they knew that I had telepathic contact with Helen, I don't think they'd be surprised. They are a friendly people with great respect for a dog my size, and they trust Ben with their airline.

***

No one in the government seemed to know that we'd been asked to help in the fight JAGS was heading to defend the islands in the Turks & Caicos Drug War. This was a war that affected everyone, but was conducted with no fanfare or publicity. Ben told us that there were no secrets in the Turks & Caicos Islands, yet this seemed to be a secret war where people were being killed, and innocents died from using contaminated drugs that were designed to kill.

JAGS knew, and even he couldn't stop the drug lords' attacks. The problem wasn't just drugs, it was also Castro smuggling fish and goods made in Cuba through South Caicos to Miami and the Russians messing with NASA's down-range radar tracking station and the US Navy space laser testing Station on Grand Turk. The people had great faith in JAGS McCartney's ability to lead their country through this quagmire of international political intrigue that was laying like a blanket over God's gift to His people.

As Ben came into the house, he asked me if I was ready for a run on the beach. Then he called out, "Helen, are you ready?"

"Just pick up the picnic basket while I get a towel to sit on," she answered.

The TCNA Administration and Accounting Offices were across the street from our home, so we stopped to tell Lionel Saunders, TCNA's Deputy Manager, where we would be in case Ben was needed. Then off we went walking toward Front Street and the pier where the barge would be docked. As we approached the pier, the barge was already being moored but we were in time to wave along with the other people who had gotten there before us.

By 1000-hours the barge had been at sea, in route from Salt Cay, for the past two hours. It's a six minute flight by TCNA plane, but by sea it was a hot, uncomfortable trip. There was no way TCNA's Islander airplanes could carry all the food and goods needed for the 400 people living on the island. Its "runway" was a straight part of the road on the north side of the island and was only 1200 feet long. The island didn't have electricity, and the only other transportation was one old pick-up truck. No large ships could dock to deliver fuel, so everything TCNA couldn't carry came by barge when the weather was right.

Ben and Kenneth "Doggy" Prospere, a businessman who owned dry cleaners and tailor shops on Grand Turk and Provo, had purchased over twenty bicycles for the island in an effort to provide more transportation options, but the salt air had rusted them away in just a few weeks. The island was so small, the Commissioner of Police didn't even have a constable stationed there. British Cable and Wireless did have a phone located in the Brown Hotel, and someone from the phone company would call once a day just to be sure the phone was working. There was an aid station with a nurse and TCNA would fly injured people out when needed.

Every morning, TCNA would fly to Salt Cay delivering mail, small supplies and passengers. Ben said it was a regularly scheduled airline route; the shortest in the world. During the rest of the day, Ben had the airline pilots turn to the right after taking off to the east and extend their crosswind leg to pass over Salt Cay. The island had no radio, so the pilot checked the section of the road used for a runway to see if there was a red panel or someone laying beside the road. If this happened, the pilot would radio the Grand Turk tower and another TCNA plane would be sent to pick them up. There was also a small 10' x 10' building used as shade for the passengers and a place to keep their bags.

There was also a nurse on the island, but no doctor. All

doctors were on Grand Turk, which had the only hospital in the Turks & Caicos Islands. Anyone needing more care than the hospital could provide was flown to Nassau in the Bahamas or Miami in the United States.

TCNA pilots used this system of fly-overs to check on the people of all the islands because most didn't have radios. During daylight hours, every island with people on it was checked at least every two hours. If someone was laying beside the landing strip and the plane had a vacant seat, the pilot would land to pick them up. If this wasn't possible, he would radio for any TCNA plane that had a vacant seat to pick up the injured person.

On the day we first visited the Brown Hotel, there were no guests and no tourists on the island. The hotel had six rooms, and its water came from a storage tank of rainwater on the roof. It also had a small electric generator that ran a refrigerator used for beer and bottled water, but there was no ice. Water was not a problem for me, because I drink rainwater like all the citizens of the Turks & Caicos Islands. Ben had bottled water flown in from Miami for himself and the rest of our clan. When we traveled to the other islands, Ben and Helen survived by drinking beer. I think most of the islanders did the same thing, even though they drank rainwater at home.

At one point, the brewer of St. Polly Girl sent one of their vice presidents in charge of advertising to see if they could advertise to get a bigger share of the beer market in Cockburn Town. It seems they were shipping as much beer to Grand Turk as was being shipped to the city of Milwaukee. Cockburn Town, the capital and largest city in the Turks & Caicos Islands, had a population of 3,500 people and one 162 dogs. (All the dogs were members of my security team, and dogs don't drink beer because we can't get the caps off the bottles or open the cans.) I think the only way St. Polly Girl could've sold more beer would have been to give every family a bathtub and advertise that it was more healthful to bathe in beer than in the ocean.

The Brown Hotel's dinning area was also the bar, and like all the hotels on Grand Turk it only served dinner if reservations were made by noon. The menu was always the same: Conch soup, conch fritters, fresh caught fish or lobster, potatoes, and pie for desert. There was no butter, bread, salad, or red meat. To make dinner reservations, you picked fish or lobster and told the headwaiter the time you wanted dinner served.

Mr. Brown then sent one of the busboys out to the beach to gather the conch and lobsters that were needed. If the reserved meal was fish, he sent word to someone going out in a fishing boat telling them what was needed. The meals were delicious. They were cooked with olive oil and served with lemon. The smallest lobsters reached from Ben's fingertips to his elbow.

Everyone was served one lobster but there was no charge if you wanted another one, you just had to wait about thirty minutes while one of the busboys ran down to the beach to catch one. I didn't have to worry about dinner because Helen had my dry dog food stored in separate plastic sandwich bags for individual servings. This way, when it was my meal time I could eat wherever we were.

Normally I eat twice a day, once in the morning before work, and then in the evening at 1700-hours. Plus, a snack whenever I can get it. This way when we are at a restaurant or a hotel, I can stay under the table and watch for the bad guys. The only thing I missed was having an apple for a treat. Ben would have apples flown in from the states for dog treats, but there was no way Helen could carry one with us when we were away from Grand Turk.

This visit was to help the Salt Cay villagers find ways to attract tourists to their island. If they could help get the island's ten guest rooms rented, the truck would be kept busy, the fishermen would have spending money, and best of all, the airline would fill all its seats on the shortest scheduled airline route in the world.

The islands are a great place to vacation — the temperature is always between 72° and 80° all year 'round. Then, it cools off at night when it rains. There are no TVs and no machinery to make noise. The normal sounds are children laughing as they play cricket in the village square. Sometimes dogs bark, but it's usually an excited short bark and they're done. There are long, beautiful, white sandy beaches meeting the warm sea water and friendly people, making this an ideal place to get away from the hustle and bustle of big city life.

The men fish during the day while the boys gather enough conch and lobster to feed everyone. They never take more than what's needed from the sea, but no one goes hungry. One man had made his house into a guest home with two bedrooms. His plan was that he and his family would sleep in the kitchen when guests were there. Their guests would have the bedrooms and eat fresh fish, lobster, and conch with his family.

The government had also built two cottages on one of the white sandy beaches and had a generator to provide electricity. This made eight bedrooms with electricity for tourists if you counted the hotel, and two without power. This was the largest industry providing cash dollars to the island since the salt business disappeared.

JAGS, the Chief Minister, worried that the Columbian drug cartels might try to take control of Salt Cay now that they were stopped from using South Caicos after the sinking the Carol "B". During one of his visits to our home on Grand Turk, I heard him tell Ben we should report any planes that landed on Salt Cay to the Commissioner of Police. It wasn't an area where the drug cartel could sell their products because the people didn't have money or the means to earn any, but if the drug cartels found some way to use the island for refueling planes he was sure that they would try to bring in drugs.

"What can we do to stop them?" Helen asked.

That was a hard question. When JAGS left, no one had been able to come up with an answer.

"Helen, have Montana alert his agents on Salt Cay and report on every plane or stranger that lands on the island. Not just for drugs but also anyone storing fuel," Ben said.

When Air Florida Airlines first came to the Turks & Caicos Islands, they landed on Grand Turk, then TCNA flew the tourists to the islands where they had reservations. If a plane from the US or Canada landed on Grand Turk, it looked like the entire population came to the airport for the fun and excitement. Liam Maguire, Minister of Tourism, hired a band to play music and dogs ran through the crowd; it became one big happy party.

Any time this happened, all the dogs would try to meet with me at the same time, and Helen would try to keep them away. A few dog fights started, but they weren't serious. The people didn't even pay any attention. I was so busy reading messages and leaving notes that I ran out of pee.

Ben told Helen it was more exciting than a barrel of

monkeys. I didn't quite understand this, since there were no monkeys and very few trees on Grand Turk. There was one large shade tree near the terminal building where most of the Haitian visitors waited for the airliners to land, but no monkeys.

***

One day a young lady in a TCNA uniform who was very excited came over to us and announced in a loud, proud voice, "We have two tourists for Salt Cay."

"That's very good. Where are they from?" Ben asked.

"They're from Quebec, Canada, and have reservations at the Guest House," she answered.

The two tourists, man and wife, smelled good and looked to be in their sixties. While Helen introduced them to me, I heard Ben tell the TCNA agent to put them on the flight to South Caicos and have the pilot drop them off on the way. She told him the plane was already overloaded, and the pilot said that even with dropping them off he would still be too heavy for takeoff on the road at Salt Cay. She started whispering asking what she should do. Ben just laughed. Then said, "Have Keith Malcolm bring out the Cessna 310. I'll fly them over to the island."

After he returned, we started walking home and Ben was laughing as he told Helen about the two visitors from Canada. After their baggage was loaded, the overcoats, gloves, and boots were laid on the seat next to the woman. Her husband sat in the copilot's seat, and as they taxied out for takeoff Ben asked how long they were going to be visiting Salt Cay. "We've paid for seven days in the sun," the man answered. Ben held up his hand indicating that he was talking to the tower, and then said, "Just a minute," then he pushed the throttles forward.

As the plane lifted off the runway Ben radioed the tower, "Grand Turk Tower this is TCNA-6 (Ben's call sign), landing Salt Cay. Out." Ben had taken off to the east, and when the plane was airborne he started turning to a crosswind leg. Upon reaching eight hundred feet he reduced power for landing while turning onto the approach for the landing strip.

"What's wrong?" the man asked. Ben told him nothing was wrong, they'd merely arrived. Then he pointed to where they would be staying.

They were flying over a long, gently curved white sand beach headed for the road when the man's wife asked "Where is the airport?"

"There's no airport, just a landing strip. It's part of the road to the beach. Someone will come out from the village to pick you up. I'll stay until you're on your way to the Guest House. It's located in the village, so you can walk everywhere."

After landing they had to wait fifteen minutes before the truck arrived. The villagers had heard them land, but the truck was busy at the village pier picking up the fish that had been caught for everyone's evening meal.

When a plane landed that meant someone would be paying American dollars for a ride to the Brown Hotel or the truck would be needed for carrying freight. If it was a tourist, it would be six dollars per person. If it was freight, it would take twice as long to reach a price as it took to deliver the items on the small island. Anyway, the locals figured it meant cash, so the fish were unloaded and the truck headed to the airstrip. Everyone would just have to eat late or eat lobster this evening.

I was getting the messages from my agents who were reading the tires of the Cessna 310 after Ben landed back on Grand Turk, and then relaying the information to me. Even if this wasn't about the drug trade it was good training.

"If you want to leave and visit another island during your stay," Ben told them as they waited, "just put your bags outside the storage building near the runway. I'll have the TCNA pilots check every day. If your bags are there, they will circle the village before landing. When you see the plane circle for landing, come to the runway. A pilot can even take you to another island where other Canadians are visiting."

"Don't worry about us, we're looking forward to the peace and quite," the man answered.

I received word from one of my cohort/agents that they had their bags near the runway on the second day, and the pilot took them to Provo for the rest of their vacation. He told Ben that the tourists said they couldn't stand the silence or understand the language. It seems that they didn't realize that everyone here spoke English with a little islander accent.

A few days after they left, Helen, Ben, and I went to the airport to check on TCNA's flight operations. While there, Ben would attend the pilots' briefing, Helen would visit the venders and people waiting for connections to the other islands and I would check messages and leave instructions for my cohort/agents.

When we arrived, there were two TCNA planes sitting in front of the terminal. Both planes were loaded, but no pilots were aboard. Ben told Helen to check with the ticket agents while we went into the airline's operations room in the hangar. The Chief Pilot, Barkley Barron, and all the other pilots were talking at the same time. Ben and I just listened for a moment before Ben spoke up. "Everyone stop talking. Barkley, why aren't the planes leaving? They're loaded and takeoff should've been fifteen minutes ago."

"We're having a bit of a problem. On the last flight from Provo yesterday the pilot passed over the runway at Middle Caicos and a red panel was beside the runway with a stretcher and a nurse waiting," Barkley said. "The plane had two seats open, so he landed. When he landed, he blew one of the tires on the left main gear. He radioed another plane that was leaving Pine Cay so it could pick up his passengers because he couldn't takeoff with them, the nurse and her patient onboard. The Pine Cay plane only had one passenger and the pilot said he would pick up the tourists. So he left the tourists there and took off with the nurse and patient. That plane returned to Grand Turk and the man was taken to the hospital."

"That's good, but what's it got to do with the planes not leaving?" Ben asked.

"The problem is, the plane from Pine Cay had engine trouble and wasn't able to land at Grand Caicos. No one picked up the tourists, so they missed their flight to Miami."

Middle Caicos, also known as Grand Caicos, has three villages but no electricity. There are 450 people and 18 dogs living in the villages. All the dogs are working as part of my intelligence network. They like the excitement, and all want to help protect their people. The dogs knew about the tourists and what was really making the pilots reluctant to take off. The runway on Middle Caicos was below the ridge and it got no wind from the ocean to blow the mosquitoes away at night, the tourists had a rough time waiting for a plane that never came.

The only shelter they had was a 10' x 10' building that has no floor or walls, just a tin roof to protect passengers from the sun or rain while they wait for a TCNA plane. A walking trail leads from the shelter up and over a ridge that joins the village's short street. All of the island's people live on the top and seaward side of the ridge, so the sea breezes keep the mosquitoes away. Unfortunately, the air is black with mosquitoes where the tourists had to wait.

There was a dead silence as Barkley spoke. Then Ben said, "You still haven't told me why the planes are still here."

"No one wants to be the pilot who has to pick up the passengers left on Middle Caicos overnight," he replied. "We know there is no way a plane can land on that airstrip at night, but they don't and they're going to be mad. They not only missed their connection to return to Miami, but the next airliner leaving Grand Turk won't be until Friday."

This is why I like to be with Ben when something like this happens. He doesn't pass the buck. "Those pilots who were off duty yesterday, hold up your hands." Then he told Barkley to assign one of these pilots to the plane delivering passengers to South Caicos. After they were dropped off, the pilot was to proceed to Middle Caicos and pick up the stranded tourists. The pilot that had the blown tire and had picked up the injured man was to take a charter flight that was scheduled for Puerto Plata.

Then Ben added, "Those are going to be two very unhappy people when they discover that there are no flights to Miami for the next two days. "Super C", reserve rooms for them at each of the hotels so everyone will be taken care of. TCNA will pick up the cost of the rooms and meals, but no drinks.

"Barkley, post the condition of the person who needed medical attention on the flight scheduling board. This way if any of the pilots are asked what happened, they can explain how our emergency medical system works. Be sure the pilots tell them about the condition of the patient.

"When that's done, Marsh, have the Cessna 310 made ready. Helen and I will be spending the next three days visiting TCNA agents and employees on the other islands."

***

Stanley Williams, the commissioner of police, kept JAGS informed about the efforts to stop the drug lords, and the movement of drugs through the islands to the United States. He was like a general who ran the battle and took the heat if things went wrong. Stanley was a good battle planner and had intelligence information coming directly to his office from Scotland Yard, US Customs agents, and he even informants within the drug cartel on the Turks & Caicos Islands.

My cohort/agents reported everything that the police commissioner learned, when it occurred, and sometimes they even knew what was going to happen before it happened. Stanley had a family dog who stayed with him except when he was working at his office. The police mascot covered this area. Mine was the only information gathering organization that the commissioner of police was never able to penetrate.

On the first of May 1980, the commissioner of police reported to JAGS that TCNA had been able to stop the shipment of drugs on all of their aircraft. Also that Customs and

Immigration officers had established procedures that required planes stopping in the islands to first land on Grand Turk, South Caicos, or Provo. Everyone, including the passengers, had to be cleared, even if the stop was only for refueling. Every plane was searched and inspected by Customs during the stop. Only airline luggage that was not unloaded missed being inspected.

This forced the drug smugglers to set up a refueling point for their planes coming from Columbia on West Caicos. The Chief Minister was so confident about winning the battle to save the islands from the drug cartels that he left for a meeting with the US State Department in the United States on the third of May to request financial assistance to keep this type of security force in place. They agreed.

***

Shortly after midnight on the ninth of May 1980, the Governor of the Turks & Caicos Islands, John Strong, contacted the Honorable Liam Maguire, Minister of Tourism, (the only government minister in the islands at that time) and informed him that a passport and documents belonging to Chief Minister JAGS McCartney, had been found in the wreckage of a Cessna 411 in Vineland, NJ.

Because of the explosion and fire that consumed the wrecked aircraft, identification of four badly-burned bodies by photograph was impossible. Nine hours had passed before anyone in the Turks & Caicos Islands even knew of the tragedy. Both the UPI and AP wire service reports were generating ponderous amounts of misinformation, leading people in the United States to believe the plane had been downed as part of a plot against the Turks & Caicos Islands.

Earl "Super C" Ingram notified Ben that the Vineland, NJ, police found a wrecked plane with papers belonging to JAGS and that they thought he was one of the victims. ("Super C" had been the personal body guard for JAGS, and headed the PDM's Action Committee before working for TCNA. JAGS had moved "Super C" to the airline and put him in charge of the baggage section in an effort to stop the movement of drugs on TCNA planes before Ben became its General Manager.)

"Super C" left to identify the body that morning. He was to meet with the British Consulate in New York and then with the US FAA to identify which one of the victims was JAGS McCartney. The US State Department assumed that JAGS was one of the passengers on the burned aircraft because of the paperwork they'd found.

Two of the other bodies had already been identified using clothing and personal effects. They were former Camden, NJ State Democratic Chairman, James Joyce, 50, and the pilot, Wayne DeBellis, 33, a former Gloucester, NJ under-sheriff.

I overheard Ben and "Super C" talking after "Super C" returned to Grand Turk. There was no doubt about the identity of the Chief Minister, but they wondered why JAGS would have the passports of his people that needed visa stamps and other official documents from the US State Department with him if he was only going to inspect some construction project James Joyce was working on. When "Super C" left the house, they had decided that the US State Department was involved in some sort of conspiracy or cover up to prevent the people on the Turks & Caicos Islands from learning what really happened.

Joyce and DeBellis were still active in the Democratic Party, but both had been convicted of jury-tampering in 1978.

Joyce was a powerful figure in New Jersey politics, and at the time of his death he was deeply involved in Senator Edward Kennedy's bid to win the Democratic nomination as a presidential candidate. In 1975, while he was still in office, he was accused of bribery and misconduct by a state grand jury. He was acquitted of these charges by members of a jury who had been bribed by DeBellis and Joyce. They were both released pending an appeal. Joyce left his position in 1976 after eight years as Democratic State Chairman. The court case hadn't been tried yet, and both were still active in the political arena.

The fourth body was a badly burned Caucasian woman. She had no identification other than her jewelry, which was very expensive. Witnesses who saw her board the Cessna 411 estimated her to be between 30 and 40 years old and said she was well dressed. They didn't know who she was with, only that she was in the co-pilot's seat when the plane took off. Everyone assumed that her body was still the only one unidentified in the accident, but my agents on South Caicos soon discovered that there were *two* unidentified bodies.

I started receiving messages on the third of June from my cohort/agents on South Caicos. They said a man was using the passport of James Joyce from Camden, NJ. He was onboard an Air Florida flight that had landed on South Caicos in route to Puerto Plata, Dominican Republic. They even reported he was 50 years old, and that he was traveling alone. JAGS had insisted that all passengers and aircraft crews landing in the Turks & Caicos Islands must disembark and pass through immigration. This practice was about to cast a light on another mystery.

When I told Helen, she phoned the TCNA's office and told

Ben that we needed him. After he heard that someone was using James Joyce's passport, he went to the USAF airbase where there was a secure military phone that could be used to call his operations center in Miami. Ben asked for a man named Dennis R. Fagan. When Ben told him about the man traveling to Puerto Plata using James Joyce's passport, he was informed that the US does not have any laws to stop someone from using his own passport.

My cohort/agent was in the USAF Base Commander's office napping when Ben made the phone call. He sent me a message saying that all Ben said when he learned this bit of information was, "I'll be dammed!"

Later, Ben told us that there were two mysteries. The first was the mystery of the two unidentified dead people. The second was the nagging question: Why had they been killed? The plane crash didn't have the markings of a drug killing because the drug cartels would've claimed responsibility because they'd want the publicity to act as a warning to others. Ben thought it had to be someone trying to interfere with the US Space Program or the US Navy's laser testing station on Grand Turk. He also wondered if it could be about Senator Edward Kennedy's campaign, which would mean it had nothing to do with the Turks & Caicos Islands.

The weekly news published by *The Green Flash* had it right when they wrote "an inference of political symbiosis is both illogical and ridiculous." They were writing about the forthcoming election between the PDM and PNP and had no way of knowing that JAGS had placed the Turks & Caicos Islands on the world stage. The US State Department was backing the United Nations' plan to use the islands as a refuge for Vietnamese Boat People and JAGS was a key player.

In April 1980, a month before the tragic death of JAGS, the Chief Minister, John Strong, the governor of the Turks & Caicos Islands, informed *The Atlantic Journal* that the United States should be ready and willing to give immediate financial aid to the Turks & Caicos Islands. He said, quote: "We look north, think north, and are Americans in every sense of the word. We are not part of the Caribbean. We are of the Atlantic. We are Americans." It was interesting that this statement was made by the governor who had been appointed by the Queen of England.

John Houseman, publisher of the local *Conch News,* said that the top PMD elected officials were already flirting with Cuba while the PNP was looking toward the Columbian Drug Cartels for more cash. Houseman, who was also president of the Turks & Caicos Islands' Chamber of Commerce, said, "It is not important where money comes from as long as no local laws are broken."

He added, quote: "Fishing and tourism are the main sources of income in these islands and the local fishermen, in an effort to catch more fish, have poured a chlorinated cleaning solution into the fishing holes along the shallow Caicos Banks. Experts believe that the fish will never return to these locations. Both fish and conch have been over-harvested."

Ben has told us many times that God saved these islands just for His people. He stocked the sea around them with food to feed His people and ordered Fuujin, the Okinawa God of Wind, to provide drinking water and to cool His people at night. Knowing this, and with my reports about a foreign organization trying to influence the government ministers against allowing NASA to use the islands in the US Space program, makes identifying these people a top priority.

John Houseman continued to write that perhaps the greatest problem in the islands was the political and racial divisiveness. John, a retired British Army Intelligence officer who served in Africa during WWII, lived with his native out-wife and son on Grand Turk. He was an intelligent man, but when he wrote about the PDM ministers making public pronouncements about throwing whites out of the islands and the concern that was causing, he was really talking about himself.

John is fond of saying that expatriates from England have an almost stereotypical patronizing attitude toward the Colonials. He tells visitors that the islanders are like children and can't govern themselves. His purpose is to sell subscriptions to *Conch News* to tourists and to support the PNP. He also uses his stories to get the attention of people at the hotel bar, then he tells them that one of the four government PDM ministers is called "The Minister of Unnatural Practices," another "Magoo," and another "Lewis the Lump." He forgets to tell them that one of the ministers is also a Scotsman.

Houseman is one of forty expatriates living in the islands and is an outspoken advocate of using drug money. I have had my agents check on every expatriate in our search for the Russian agents, and we have identified seven men who support using the drug cartel's money.

***

Items in the news after the plane crash was reported:

• *Foreign Exchange,* another small monthly paper that welcomes queries about historical facts about the islands and any news that relates to tourism, reported that the plans to send their representative to the 1980 Miss Universe Beauty

Pageant in Korea that July had not been canceled after the crash was reported. Miss Constance Lightbourne, an 18 year old inter-island queen from South Caicos was to leave on 14th June for the rehearsals and pre-competition briefings. She was the Turks & Caicos Islands' first representative in an international beauty contest. Her gown was a striking interpretation of a South Caicos lobster.

• John Houseman was replaced as president of the Chamber of Commerce by Charles Mesick, the senior partner in the accounting firm of Mesick and Associates based in Provo.

• The US Navy Base on Grand Turk was leased to the Tourist Board and renamed McCartney Resort Village.

• Governor John Strong notified the PMD that they had no more authority than any member of the PNP on the 9th of May. The Executive Council moved out of their offices on the 11th of May and a democratic form of government for the Turks & Caicos Islands ceased to exist.

• It was also discovered that the Governor may have acted prematurely in declaring the seat and office of the Chief Minister vacant. It was the 23rd of May before the remains were medically identified making JAGS officially dead.

A week later we learned that James Joyce wasn't killed in the crash of the Cessna-411.

***

Sometimes in the evenings, Helen and I would take Ben for a walk on the beach along Front Street and he would tell us about what was happening on all of the islands that TCNA checks on every day. Ben was telling us about an island called West Caicos. No people or dogs live on this island, yet it has a 3500 foot airstrip that's in moderate condition. This island should have been an ideal place to live, since it had the same arid climate and sparse vegetation of the eastern islands of the Turks & Caicos and no water. The sun was known to shine there for 350 days a year and climatically West Caicos is considered to be a Salt Island.

West Caicos Island is 7 miles long and 2 miles wide, and is located five miles from South Bluffs on Providenciales. The island is flat, and scrub brush covers the ground. The depth of the ocean on the west side is over 7500 feet and ships can approach within fifty feet of the land. The water on the east side facing toward the Caicos Banks is very shallow, with a pass named Caicos Creek suitable for small sail boats. West Caicos has only one small white sand beach of about 200 feet on the south end of the island. This island is unique due to the abrupt cliff shoreline on the western lee side that some say makes an ideal site for a prison. The island has a primitive road system but no people, houses or white sandy beaches and the ocean here is full of hammerhead sharks, especially on the east side in the Caicos Banks.

Liam Maguire is a professional surveyor who has been involved in real estate and development projects in the Turks & Caicos Islands for over twenty years and is interested in this island. A ship-to-ship fuel transfer operation was established there in 1980 off the west side of the island, and permanent facilities were to be built on a 25 acre site on the north-western part of the island. In the south-eastern area 100 acres were transferred to a developer, but no work was started.

Twenty-seven years later seven Israeli Contractors started to build a hotel complex there that looked more like a prison than a resort. Their plan may have been to lease the hotel and West Caicos complex to the Jewish government in Israel as a prison to house captured terrorists. The American Military Prison at Guantanamo, Cuba, was about a 100 miles from West Caicos. If the United States closed this prison they just might pay Israel to house the terrorist prisoners to avoid moving them into the United States.

A Jewish prison might also help solve the problem of how to stop the recruitment of terrorists. During WWII, the United States discovered that the Kamikaze pilots who killed themselves while fighting Americans had been recruited from Shinto Shrines. To stop the Japanese from volunteering as Kamikaze pilots, President Truman outlawed the religion and closed the shrines when the Japanese surrendered. Today terrorists are recruited in Muslim Mosques, and believe that they will go to heaven and receive 72 virgins if they kill Christian men, women, and children. To stop the terrorists and re-educate them may require that these modern day terrorists not be allowed to practice the Muslim religion while incarcerated.

***

Stanley Williams, Commissioner of Police, had the West Caicos airstrip checked every day around 1700 hours. If drums of aviation gas were stored beside the runway he would have the fuel picked up by a local charter plane and taken to Provo. The fuel was given to TCNA and my cohort/agents reported that the fuel was added to the airport fuel storage tanks. A receipt would be issued for the gallons received, and only the airline could use the fuel.

The reason for the 1700 hours (5:00 PM) fly-over was to be sure that it would be dark before the drug planes arrived from Columbia. There was no way to get more fuel to West Caicos after darkness had fallen, so the drug planes would have to go to South Caicos for fuel. The Police would be waiting for them there. No drug plane was ever seized until it was fueled and the gasoline was paid for. This way, everyone got their money. When the police seized the plane afterwards, the court fined the pilot $5000 US dollars plus kept the drugs and the fueled plane.

***

At 1700-hours "Super C" knocked on the door and came in with some news about a government meeting on North Caicos. I know the time because that's when Helen and Ben have supper and I practice laying under the table so I'll remember how to act when we eat at a fancy restaurant. It was a month after JAGS died and was laid to rest on PDM property next to the Airport Road. Actually, it was 15 June 1980 and the meeting was so secret that my cohort/agents had not learned of it, so "Super C" brought news that came as a complete surprise to everyone.

He told about how one of the TCNA pilots returning from Provo had picked up a passenger who was going from Pine Cay to North Caicos. When he landed at North Caicos, there was a Cuban DC-6 parked on the ramp and Cuban military soldiers were guarding the plane. The TCNA pilot asked the cab drivers where the meeting was and who was invited. He learned that the new Chief Minister of the PDM, Oswald Skippings, and all the ministers of the Turks & Caicos Islands (except for Liam Maguire who had announced that he was not going to run again) were meeting with representatives of the Cuban government at one of the villages.

It was suppertime, so if they left now Ben and "Super C" could be at the airport on North Caicos before dark. They had to get there before dark because the taxicab would leave then.

(There was no electricity on the island yet and nothing much happened after dark.) Ben told us that he would be back the next day. He would be staying overnight at the Whitby Hotel on North Caicos. Then they left.

I think they ran all the way to the airport and rolled out the Cessna-310 by themselves. I heard "Super C" tell Ben that he could get the people on north Caicos to help him when they got there, but it was up to Ben to get the Cuban's to cooperate.

There was no way I could send a message about what was happening on North Caicos to my cohort/agents. To my surprise, though, I started receiving messages from all the tires of planes telling about the meeting and what was happening to "Super C" and Ben.

When the Cessna-310 landed, there were two twin-engine charter aircraft parked on the ramp in front of the terminal building. One was based in Grand Turk and the other was from Provo. Ben parked TCNA's Cessna-310 next to them and walked across the ramp to the Cuban DC-6. He asked the Cuban guard if he could speak to his Sergeant. Instead, a Cuban man in a business suit came down the steps of the plane to meet Ben. Meanwhile, "Super C" found the taxi driver and hired him for the rest of the day. This way, no matter what happened, they would have transportation.

Ben was talking to the Cuban in the suit who spoke nearly perfect English. Ben said, "I'm the General Manager of TCNA and this is "Super C", the head of security for the PDM. I was brought here at the request of the Chief Minister's security police. I have information that the Chief Minister has sent for. You may check my credentials with the Honorable Liam Maguire." Ben knew that Liam was not at the meeting, and that he had the Turks & Caicos government give the Cubans 10 acres of land at the South Caicos Airport for their smuggling operation. Ben was guessing that the Cubans wouldn't know that Liam was on his way out of power. He also hoped they would want to remain on friendly terms.

He was right. A Cuban plain clothes secret police officer told Ben they would contact someone at the meeting site via radio and inform them that Ben and "Super C" would arrive within the hour. They were lucky, since the New Chief Minister, the Honorable Oswald Skippings, and the Minister of Labor, the Honorable Lewis Astwood, did not like Castro's Communist representatives, but they both knew Ben and trusted him. When the New Chief Minister was given the message by the Cuban radio operator, Oswald Skippings turned to Lewis and said, "It's about time they got here."

Later, Ben told us that he didn't know whether the Cubans had believed him or not. But figured they had when they started calling him "sir." The Cuban secret police officer informed them that he was in charge of the Cuban's security team, then introduced a Russian as his assistant. They believed that the communists knew JAGS McCartney's death was actually an assassination. They didn't express any emotion whatsoever, though.

When "Super C" had identified JAGS's body, he asked the coroner why the body's feet weren't burned. The coroner told them that the person may have been laying on the floor of the baggage compartment with his feet toward the tail of the aircraft when it burned. "Super C" had put body bags in this position in the Cessna-310 before, so Ben could carry three large people and the body to a funeral on the deceased's home island. (There was no mortuary in the islands and a person's body had to be buried the day he or she died.) This made him think that had been the position JAGS was in when the plane crashed.

"Super C" and Ben had both agreed that JAGS must've been assassinated before he was placed on the plane. Another item that pointed in this direction was that all the official documents of the US State Department said his personal luggage was also on the plane. They knew that documents can be changed since they are only paper, *and* James Joyce, formerly presumed dead in the crash, was still alive.

There was also the fact that the governor had been misled or ill-advised by the three practicing attorneys in Cockburn Town, and this caused the Turks & Caicos Islands to be without a government for over thirty days. What really happened during this thirty days may never be known, but what happened at the meeting on North Caicos is known by the people who were there.

The Cuban and Russian security agents climbed into the taxi with "Super C" and Ben. The "taxi" was an old Ford station wagon. "Super C" gave instructions to the driver about how to find the turnoff for the village and warned him about a bump in the narrow road ahead. It was dark and only the vehicle's lights showed the dirt road as it twisted and turned. Ben told us that "Super C" was such a good actor that even he began to believe the story they'd told the Cuban security officer.

When they arrived there were two bonfires burning. They were separated by about twenty feet and were being used for light to see by. There were two rows of logs the length of the distance between the bonfires facing two rows of logs where the Cuban representative sat. Ben counted three Cubans on the first log and seven others behind them on the other log. When Ben approached, one of the Cubans was speaking and Oswald Skippings just nodded before he stood up, and without saying a word, shook Ben's hand. Then he directed Ben to sit between him and Lewis Astwood. Lewis scooted over and Ben sat down. Not a word had been spoken, but the Cuban who was speaking got so confused he stopped talking and just stood there.

There is one thing every British parliamentarian knows and that is how to debate in the parliamentary arena. Skippings may not have known what the Cubans' agenda was, but he knew how to confuse them and change the subject.

One of my agents sent a message saying that until Ben showed up he'd been napping because nothing was worth reporting. When Ben sat down between Oswald and Lewis, everyone started shouting out their opinions. In fact, some of the dogs started barking and running around, too. It was turning into a real political meeting.

"Super C" had stopped to talk with the village elders while Ben made his entrance. When things started too calm down "Super C" shouted insults about the Russian KGB, the US CIA and even the US State Department.

Skippings (2nd Minister), Lewis (3rd Minister), and Ben had their heads together so no one could hear them, and Oswald asked about the message he was carrying. Ben told him that this meeting was taking place only because JAGS had been assassinated and the Russians thought that they could now control the PDM.

Lewis told him, "We've gone too far and can't stop now."

"Give me permission to speak on behalf of the people,"

Ben said, "and then listen to what I have to say." Then he left the log and joined "Super C" in the shadows.

Oswald Skippings proved that he was the Chief Minister and leader of the PDM that night. He told those at the meeting that Ben wanted to speak, but the Cubans said it shouldn't be allowed because Ben was an American and it was against United States law for a citizen of the US to speak for the US State Department. Oswald argued that Ben was not speaking for the United States, but for the people of the Turks & Caicos Islands.

When the fight finally settled down, the Cubans agreed that Ben could speak but only after every Cuban representative had finished. Skippings and the Ministers agreed to this if the Cubans agreed that the meeting would not be closed until Ben had a chance to speak.

Two hours later, Ben was given permission to speak. He started by thanking the Turks & Caicos Islands' ministers for letting him speak since he was a man with dual residency. He acknowledged that he was not speaking for the United States, but as a person who had lost a friend. I don't know the exact words — if you have ever tried to read messages from a dog who has peed upon a plane's tire then you know the problems involved — but the following is the is a good representation.

Ben told how "Super C" had learned that JAGS was dead and had been assassinated before the plane had crashed, as well as how they'd discovered that James Joyce was not on the plane at all. From the very moment he started to speak, he treated the Cubans as if they were the Royal Opposition and only addressed the Turks & Caicos Islands' Government Ministers.

He explained how Governor Strong claimed the Turks & Caicos Islands people were Americans, and told them about the Honorable Henry Bowings' statement that JAGS McCartney was the first National Hero of the Turks & Caicos Islands, as reported in the *The Green Flash.* He said that statement was totally correct.

He told them that three decades from today all their children *could* be born Americans. Also that they could approve laws that would allow US hospitals in New York or Miami to help with the births of their children. They could even require that every mother must live near the hospital for 30 days before a child was born and that the crown must pay for the airfare of the fathers so they could stay with the child's mother in the United States.

Everyone began taking part in the debate, and the villagers were clapping and the dogs were barking as Ben finished. "I believe that this was part of the plan JAGS was working on," he told them. "If the Cubans are allowed to interfere with the plan, then we have turned our backs upon a National Hero who was assassinated because he believed that God created these islands for his people."

Ben then walked over to Super "C" and they walked over to the taxi and got in. They left the debate in Skippings' hands and headed to the hotel. The next morning during breakfast they learned that the Cubans had left at daybreak and NASA had their down-range station.

DEATH OF A PATRIOT HISTORICAL DOCUMENTS

The following documents are used by the author to help verify the historical facts. This book is based on the nonfiction adventure of the Games Clan during the Turks & Caicos Islands' secret drug war.

This story was not written to change history, only to record what the Patriots of the Turks & Caicos Islands did to protect the land of their birth from the drug cartels. For those students of history who disagree or who just can't believe that JAGS McCartney was assassinated in 1980, I suggest a visit to the islands so you can ask "Super C" what really happened. Ask him if it was because the Columbian drug cartels were attempting to make South Caicos into a international flea market for drug dealers. Or if it was the need to expand Cuban communist smuggling operations, or was it an attempt by Russian communists to interfere with the United States space program? Skeptics should visit Grand Turk and start by asking the people who were there, then study the Bible's book of Genesis and these historical documents to verify for themselves what part is historical fact and what part may be conjecture.

The author called this period "The Secret Islands Drug War" when writing in his journals about the Games Clan's work for JAGS McCartney, Chief Minister of the Turks & Caicos Islands. The United States treated the action as a part of the US Customs control of Cuban smuggling operations, and the control of drug traffic. The British treated it as a local police action and Scotland Yard considered it a drug control problem. The British Foreign Office and the US CIA treated it as a political problem between the US and Russia for the control of space. It seems that only JAGS McCartney knew that it was really a war that would affect the world.

Today we know that JAGS was more than just the Chief Minister and leader of a small island nation, he also a man who saved God's islands for his people. He helped put the first man on the moon by providing a base on Grand Turk for the Americans to develop their first NASA down-range station and while his small country remained part of the British Empire. His skill at juggling nations to protect the islands' interests with only a handful of police to help him was an outstanding political achievement.

Montana and brother, Starr.

CREDITS

Credit for the adventure story *Death of a Patriot* must be given to all the men and women who worked in the shadows to preserve the jewels of the Caribbean for the Turks & Caicos Islands' people.

A special thanks to Harry Alexander, OSS, who taught the author about the need for gathering intelligence. Also to the fine men and women of the Southeastern Guide Dogs School of Palmetto, Florida, who helped Montana learn his trade. Without Montana's Guide Dog skills, dedication, and the loyalty of the Turks & Caicos Islands' dogs, many more could have died.

Thanks to the dedication of men and women like Earl C. Ingram ("Super C"), Kenneth Prospere (Doggy), Lewis Astwood, Stanley E. Williams, Barkley Barron, James Bassett, Marsh Green, Carol Brooks, Chris Coriat, Edward Bruce, and all of the men and women working for the Turks & Caicos Islands National Airline (TCNA) who inspired the author to write about the Patriot JAGS McCartney.

Please add the name of anyone you know who worked for TCNA during 1980 or helped in the war against the drug cartels. They are truly Patriots of the Turks & Caicos Islands, BWI.

_____

_____

FUUJIN FORWARD

Reference: Picture of Fuujin, Okinawa God of Wind. Emblem of the 4th Fighter Squadron during the Korean War,

FUUJIN, the Okinawa God of Wind, green, carrying a large yellow sack, wearing a red scarf draped about the neck and shoulders, all in front of a gray thunder cloud with yellow lighting flash and raindrops issuing towards a dexter base. Approved as an Emblem of the 4th Fighter Squadron by the USAF on 25 February 1949.

Ben R. Games, 1st Lt. USAF was a fighter pilot flying the P-61s & F-82G in the 4th Fighter Squadron in 1949/50.

4th FIGHTER SQUADRON LINEAGE

Constituted the 4th Pursuit Squadron on 20 Nov 1940, Activated on 15 Jan 1941. Redesignated: 4th Fighter Squadron 15 May 1942. Inactivated 7 Nov 1945, Activated on 20 Feb 1947. Redesignated: 4th Fighter Squadron (All Weather) on 10 Aug 1948; 4th Fighter Squadron All Weather on 20 Jan 1950; 4th Fighter-Interception Squadron on 25 Apr 1951.

During WW-II. Combat Operations ETO & MTO. Campaigns, Air Offensive, Europe, Algeria-French Morocco, Tunisia, Sicily, Naples Apennines; Rhineland; Central Europe; Po Valley; Air Combat EAME Theater. Aircraft: P-40, P-39, Spitfire, and P-51.

Stations during 1949 & 1950; Naha, Okinawa & Misawa, Japan. Aircraft assigned during this period P-61 and F-82G. Operations. Combat Air defense of the Ryukyus Islands during the Korean War.

FUUJIN

by Ben R. Games, PhD

The Great One created the Heaven and Earth. Then he built a Garden of Eden for his likeness. Then he rested. The next day he looked down upon his garden and saw that the trees, flowers, and meadows needed water for they were turning brown; so he created soft billowy clouds to rain upon them. Then he looked down again and saw that the ground had too much water and was turning into mud. God called the Archangel Michael and told him to think of some way to help His garden grow.

The Archangel formed a committee of Angels and told them that the Lord had said to help the garden grow. They decided that someone would have to move the clouds to where the rain was needed, help pollinate the flowers, and help to spread the seeds of all the plants. When the Lord heard of the plan he called out, "FUUJIN."

"On warm days I gently rock the baby's cradle, dry the sweat from the man's brow, and move the clouds where they are needed to water the crops. I help move ships, and make high waves for the surfers. I help powered parachutes and trikes fly. I even help sail boats win races. I make dust devils in dry fields and play with leaves in the fall. I am FUUJIN.

Upon God's order I moved the waters of the Red Sea. I can change the shape of mountains, and create floods. I am on duty all the time. I seldom rest and I can change the winner of sail boat races just for fun. I can destroy crops, towns, or just one building. I can make a fisherman laugh or cry. I am FUUJIN.

Some call me Typhoon, Hurricane, Tornado, Chinook, Thor, but no matter what I am called everyone knows me, loves me, hates me, and fears me. I am in charge of making the clouds move, and in helping God's children take care of the earth. I am the Okinawa God of Wind. I am FUUJIN.

REPRINTED FROM JANUARY 1980

AMÉRICAS

Turks & Caicos Islands

"The kind of Caribbean paradise many travelers are looking for"

Cockburn Town on Grand Turk Island

Turks & Caicos Tourist Board
P.O. Box 592617
Miami, Florida 33159
(305) 592-6183

Américas magazine is published by the General Secretariat
of the Organization of American States, Washington, DC 20006

Turks & Caicos Islands

Information

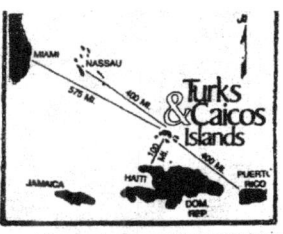

FOR INFORMATION AND ASSISTANCE IN HOTEL RESERVATIONS

CONTACT: Turks and Caicos Tourist Board, (305) 592 6183

MIAMI
NASSAU
575 MI.
400 MI.
Turks & Caicos Islands
JAMAICA
HAITI
DOM. REP.
PUERTO RICO

FLY AIR FLORIDA

Bahamasair

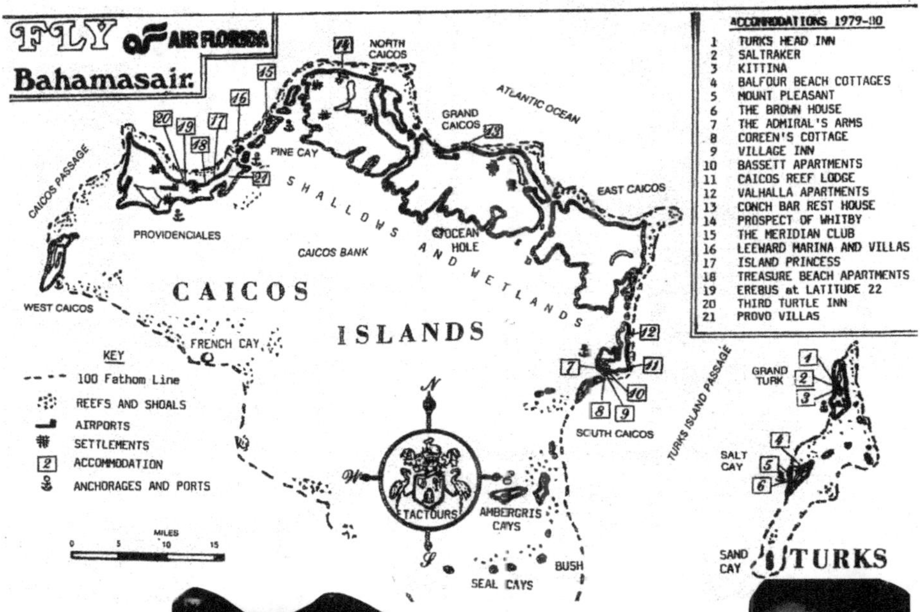

NORTH CAICOS
ATLANTIC OCEAN
GRAND CAICOS
PINE CAY
CAICOS PASSAGE
PROVIDENCIALES
SHALLOWS AND WETLANDS
OCEAN HOLE
CAICOS BANK
EAST CAICOS
WEST CAICOS
CAICOS
ISLANDS
FRENCH CAY
SOUTH CAICOS
TURKS ISLAND PASSAGE
GRAND TURK
SALT CAY
AMBERGRIS CAYS
TACTOURS
BUSH
SEAL CAYS
SAND CAY
TURKS
KEY
100 Fathom Line
REEFS AND SHOALS
AIRPORTS
SETTLEMENTS
ACCOMMODATION
ANCHORAGES AND PORTS
MILES
0 5 10 15

ACCOMMODATIONS 1979-80

1 TURKS HEAD INN
2 SALTRAKER
3 KITTINA
4 BALFOUR BEACH COTTAGES
5 MOUNT PLEASANT
6 THE BROWN HOUSE
7 THE ADMIRAL'S ARMS
8 COREEN'S COTTAGE
9 VILLAGE INN
10 BASSETT APARTMENTS
11 CAICOS REEF LODGE
12 VALHALLA APARTMENTS
13 CONCH BAR REST HOUSE
14 PROSPECT OF WHITBY
15 THE MERIDIAN CLUB
16 LEEWARD MARINA AND VILLAS
17 ISLAND PRINCESS
18 TREASURE BEACH APARTMENTS
19 EREBUS at LATITUDE 22
20 THIRD TURTLE INN
21 PROVO VILLAS

SOUTHEASTE
GUIDE

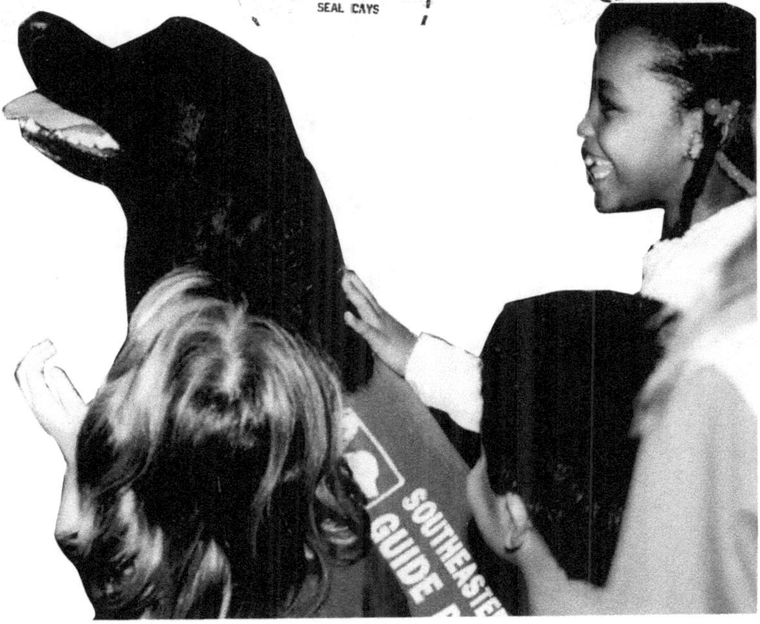

*On the Occasion of the Official Birthday
of Her Majesty Queen Elizabeth 11
His Excellency the Governor & Mrs. Strong
request the pleasure of the company of*

Mr. & Mrs B. Games.

*to a Reception
on Saturday 14th June 1980
6.30 p.m. to 8.00 p.m.*

Dress: Informal.

*Goverment House
Grand Turk.*

Lewis Astwood, Minister of
Labor (1980), Mildred
Astwood and Helen Games,
MBA

Donkey cart.

Kenneth Prospere's Tailor
Shop on Grand Turk (1980).

THE GREEN FLASH

Published by: DON CAY ASSOCIATES, GRAND TURK   June 1980   Vol.1 No.12

Turks & Caicos Mourns Loss of JAGS McCartney

ABOVE: (Left)The funeral procession arrives at the Parade Grounds on Grand Turk for the memorial service. (Right) The Chief Minister and colleagues prior to his departure for talks with the U.S. State Department in Washington, D.C. on May 3.

MEMORIAL SERVICES FOR THE LATE CHIEF MINISTER, Hon. James Alexander George Smith McCartney were conducted on Sunday, May 25 on Grand Turk. The first Chief Minister in the history of the Turks & Caicos Islands, generally known as "Jags," Mr. McCartney, 34, was killed in the crash of a private plane near Vineland, New Jersey, on May 9.

A crowd estimated at 3,500 attended the state funeral, including a six-member delegation from the Bahamas' PLP party headed by Hon. Alfred Maycock, Minister of State. Representatives from the U.S. State Dept., Canadian High Commission in Jamaica and many Turks Islanders living overseas arrived in Grand Turk May 24 for the services. Messages of sympathy were sent by hundreds of others.

The funeral cortege, which stretched for over a mile, comprised an estimated 1,000 mourners, including the official honor guard of members of the Turks & Caicos Police Force, Benevolent Association, Sea Scouts, Girl Guides and youth group bands.

During the two-hour service, a number of dignitaries paid tribute to the late Chief Minister. Speeches were made by Hon. Oswald Skippings, leader and one of the founders of the PDM party; Hon. Norman Saunders, leader of the oppostion PNP party and His Excellency the Governor, Mr. John Strong. Hon. Alfred Maycock cited the late Chief Minister's "untiring efforts to lead the Turks

THE GREEN FLASH

Turks & Caicos Islands

Published by: DON CAY ASSOCIATES, GRAND TURK

July 1980 Vol. 2 No. 1

Oswald Skippings Elected New Chief Minister

HON. OSWALD SKIPPINGS is the newly-elected Chief Minister of the Turks & Caicos Islands. Mr. Skippings, 26, was Minister of Health, Education and Welfare and Deputy Chief Minister during the late Hon. J.A.G.S. McCartney's term of office, and one of the co-founders of the People's Democratic Movement (PDM).

The June 12 by-election on Grand Turk, to fill the seat left vacant by the May 9 death of Hon. McCartney, was won by Herbert Been, who defeated his PNP opponent Richard Williams by a vote of 161-88. Mr. Been, 26, was employed as a medical lab technician at Grand Turk Hospital, and has been appointed Minister of Health, Education & Welfare.

The by-election restored the PDM's one vote majority in the Legislative Council, which again has a 6-5 (PDM to PNP) ratio.

Following Mr. Skippings' election as Chief Minister during the June 17 LEGCO session, remaining Ministerial appointments were made. Along with Mr. Been, cabinet members include Hon. C.W. Maguire, Minister of Tourism & Development, and Hon. Lewis Astwood, Minister of Works, Utilities & Labour.

No date has been set for the 1980 General Election which will take place sometime this fall.

Shown above is the new cabinet. At left, Hon. Oswald Skippings congratulates Hon. Herbert Been on his appointment as a Minister. Right: Hon. Liam Maguire(far left) and Hon. Lewis Astwood (far Right) join the Chief MInister and Hon. Been.

THE GREEN FLASH

Published by: DON CAY ASSOCIATES, GRAND TURK   September 1980   Vol. 2 No. 3

PDM, PNP Leaders Prepare for 1980 General Election

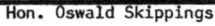

Hon. Oswald Skippings

Hon. Norman Saunders

NO OFFICIAL DATE HAS BEEN SET for the 1980 general election, but the existting Legislative Council must be dissolved by October 6. The People's Democratic Movement held its Fourth Annual Convention at McCartney Resort Village on Grand Turk, August 27-31 and during the annual general meeting, Chief Minister and PDM leader Hon. Oswald Skippings announced later, a resolution was unanimously passed by his party pledging to the electorate that the PDM is committed to a Constitutional change which would bring about full internal self-government immediately. However, the PDM now states that it cannot now accept the deadline for independence by June 1982 as set by the British Government in November 1979, unless the Turks & Caicos populace expresses approval through a referendum.

THE PROGRESSIVE NATIONAL PARTY (PNP) still plans to campaign on an anti-independence platform, says Opposition leader Hon. Norman Saunders, despite the modification of the PDM party's platform to include a referendum, because the PNP believes that the issue of independence should be resolved by the voters during the coming election, by their choice of government leaders. The PNP will not hold an annual convention, Mr. Saunders said, but will campaign by visiting each constituency and holding public meetings. The primary reason for this, he said, is that the existing government "refused to allow the PNP use of air time on the government-operated Radio Turks & Caicos, leaving us no alternatives." Chief Minister Skippings called the accusation "completely untrue."

Turks & Caicos Islands

THE GREEN FLASH

Published by: DON CAY ASSOCIATES, GRAND TURK   November 1980   Vol.2   No.5

PNP Wins Election with 8 Seats

NEW PNP GOVERNMENT MINISTERS:

Newly elected Chief Minister Norman Saunders appears at left with his cabinet. Left to right: Hon. Stafford Missick; Hon. N.J.S. Francis; Hon. Norman Saunders and Hon. Robert S. Hall. Other photos appear on page three inside.

HON. NORMAN B. SAUNDERS, MLC from South Caicos(North) became the third Chief Minister in the history of the Turks & Caicos Islands on Nov. 6, following a landslide victory by the Progressive National Party (PNP) during the Nov. 4 general election.

The PNP claimed eight of the 11 seats in the Legislative Council following a month long campaign season during which both political parties, the PNP and the former majority party, the Peoples Democratice Movement (PDM) predicted victory.

Mr. Saunders was elected Chief Minister by an 8-3 majority during the Nov. 6 meeting of the Legislative Council, defeating Hon. Oswald Skippings of Grand Turk (former Chief Minister and now Leader of the Opposition PDM Party) the other nominee.

Only Hon. Oswald Skippings and Hon. Lewis Astwood, Grand Turk candidates, were returned to thier seats in the Legislative Council to represent the PDM party. Mr. Astwood is the former Minister for Works, Utilities & Labour. The third PDM seat was won by Larry Coalbrooke, also representing a Grand Turk district. Former Minister for Tourism & Development, Liam Maguire, announced im early October that he would not seek re-election in this year's contest.

This year's election resulted in a Caicos bloc for the PNP, which claimed all seats for the Caicos Islands by returning three previously-elected representatives and sweeping the remaining three seats. The PNP also won the Salt Cay seat and recaptured its one seat on Grand Turk.

At press time, the exact Ministerial portfolios had not been announced, but the Chief Minister has appointed the remaining three Ministers: Hon. Stafford Missick (Bottle Creek, North Caicos); Hon. N.J.S. Francis (Grand Turk) and Hon.

Videotape shows island official accepting drug payoff money

MIAMI (UPI) — A videotape showing the prime minister of the Turks and Caicos Islands stuffing $20,000 in drug payoff money into his pockets was the subject of a hearing Thursday in federal court.

U.S. Magistrate Herbert Shapiro scheduled the hearing to determine whether to release portions of the two-hour videotape to the media. Defense attorneys said releasing the tape would prevent Prime Minister Norman Saunders from receiving a fair trial.

After watching the tapes, a federal magistrate Wednesday refused to reduce Saunders' $2 million bond. But Shapiro said he would lower bond for Saunders and two other island officials if the British government could guarantee they would appear for trial in Miami on narcotics conspiracy charges.

Saunders, 41, was arrested in Miami Tuesday with Stafford Missick, 47, the islands' minister of commerce and development; Aulden "Smokey" Smith, 33, parliamentary secretary to the ministry of works; and Canadian businessman Andre Fournier, 46, who now lives in Exuma, Bahamas.

Saunders has been under pressure from Great Britain to resign as chief minister of the self-governing British possession. Opposition leaders in the West Indian islands also called for his resignation and the immediate election of a new government.

Portions of a two-hour videotape, played in court by Assistant U.S. Attorney Richard Gregory, showed Saunders accepting $20,000 from an undercover agent, counting the money and stuffing $5,000 into each

Bond has been set at $2 million for Norman Saunders, the prime minister of the Turks and Caicos Islands. He and three others face narcotics conspiracy charges.

of his pockets.

One part of the tape showed the four defendants discussing a plan to set aside 10 percent of the alleged drug payoffs to be used as an emergency bail fund, enabling them to post bond and flee to Colombia if they were caught.

Bond was set at $2 million for Saunders, $1 million each for Missick and Smith, and $5 million for Fournier. All four remained jailed.

They were arrested Tuesday after meeting at a Miami hotel with federal undercover agents and charged with a variety of conspiracy offenses involving racketeering and the importation of cocaine and marijuana into the United States. The men face up to 30 years in prison if convicted, said Stanley Marcus, U.S. attorney for the Southern District of Florida.

The charges result from an alleged plot to use the Turks and Caicos Islands as a safe haven to shuttle 800 kilograms of cocaine a week from South America into the United States, said Peter Gruden, special agent in charge of the Drug Enforcement Administration office in Miami.

No cocaine had been transported, but all four defendants had accepted payments totalling $52,000 since early January, Gruden said.

On the videotape, Saunders told a DEA agent and an informant he

could provide smugglers with protection from police, Customs officers and airport officials.

Defense attorney David Roth contended U.S. agents encouraged Saunders to take part in the scheme.

"There are parts of the tape that indicate encouragement of involvement by the government, despite some resistance by my client," Roth said.

Shapiro replied that no one appeared to force Saunders to stuff the money into his pockets.

Shapiro scheduled another bond hearing for 10 a.m. Monday, and a preliminary hearing for March 15.

A British spokesman said the governor, Christopher Turner, appointed by Queen Elizabeth II, has no power to dismiss the suspected officials, who can only be ousted by the islands' ruling legislative council.

A government official in Grand Turk said Deputy Chief Minister N.J.S. "Bops" Francis had met with the governor regarding his becoming acting chief minister if Saunders resigned.

Saunders was elected to his second term as chief minister when his Progressive National Party won eight of 11 seats in elections for legislative council May 29, 1984, and has done much to promote the islands as a tourist destination and an offshore banking center.

FOREIGN CORPORATIONS

A corporation formed outside the Islands but wishing to trade within the Islands (whether such trade be domestic or offshore) must within 1 month of commencing business file with the Registrar of Companies a certified copy of its Memorandum and Articles of Association (or its equivalent), and a copy of its certificate of incorporation (or its equivalent), together with the name of one or more persons resident within the Islands to accept service of notices. A fee of $110.00 is payable upon such registration.

PARTNERSHIPS

Partnerships are governed by English Common Law.

BANKING AND FINANCIAL INSTITUTIONS

The current legislation governing the incorporation and maintenance of banks and financial institutions is The Banking Ordinance 1979. The Banking Ordinance creates two classes of banks, a class "A" bank which relates only to domestic banking within the Islands and a class "B" bank, which relates only to offshore banking operations. Nothing prevents a holder of a class "A" Licence also holding a class "B" Licence. The use of the word "Bank" may be included in a banking company's name. The minimum paid up share capital together with unimpaired reserves of a bank incorporated in the Islands is US$ 500,000 The minimum is $2,000,000.00 if the bank is incorporated outside the Islands.

The Banking Ordinance also creates a second category of Licence – namely "a financial institution". A financial institution may not use the word "bank" in its title or published literature or documents, but may conduct banking business. It must have a paid up share capital and unimpaired reserves of not less than $125,000.00 if its head office is located within the Islands or $500,000.00 if its head office is located outside the Islands.

Careful scrutiny is given to all applications for banking licences. Enquiries and references are called for in respect of all promoters, directors, shareholders and senior employees and the Foreign and Commonwealth Office in London, with the assistance of the Bank of England, render assistance to the Islands' Authorities in checking out applications for banking licences.

Following incorporation and grant of a licence under the Banking Ordinance 1979 it is possible (under the International Financial Institution (Exemptions) Ordinance 1979) to come to a negotiated agreement with the Government that the prevailing tax free advantages and free movement of assets will continue to remain unchanged and will not be varied or modified for a specific number of years.

UNIT TRUSTS, MUTUAL FUNDS, INSURANCE COMPANIES

There is no legislation relating to these activities. It is not Government policy to interfere with the free conduct of bona fide business.

SECRECY

The Confidential Relationships Ordinance 1979 imposes complete secrecy and confidentiality on the part of anyone in possession of confidential information howsoever obtained and provides severe legal sanctions for the breach of express or implied conditions of professional or commercial confidence.

INCOLEX

INCOLEX is a company incorporated under the laws of the Turks & Caicos Islands having its head office located on Grand Turk, but with representative offices located in various parts of the world.

INCOLEX was formed as a result of a request made to a consortium of lawyers, accountants and fiscalists by the Government of the Islands to establish and promote the Islands as a modern Tax Haven free of the social, political and financial difficulties which have been encountered in many other tax havens.

HEAD OFFICE
for further information or instructions
please write to:
INCOLEX
PMB 9 "The Fortress", Pond Street, Grand Turk
Turks & Caicos Islands, B.W. Indies
Telephone: Grand Turk 2533
(UK direct dialing code: 0101 809 946)
Telex: 8224 INCOLEX TQ

INCOLEX
International Corporate and Legal Services Limited
"The Fortress", PMB 9, Grand Turk
Turks & Caicos Islands, British West Indies
Telephone: (809 946) 2533
Telex: 8224 INCOLEX TQ

LEGAL SYSTEM

English Common Law is the underlying law of the Islands, modified by local Ordinances (which have to receive the approval of the British Government upon the recommendation of the Governor before passing into law). INCOLEX has played an important role in the development of various Ordinances relating to:-

Banking
Exemptions for Financial Institutions
Confidential Relationships (Secrecy)

INCOLEX has advised the Government on the contents of a new piece of legislation known as "International Companies Registration and Certification Ordinance". Additionally, INCOLEX has made recommendations for certain amendments to the Companies Ordinance 1971 (which is broadly based upon the United Kingdom Companies Act – but in a much simplified form) to improve company incorporations and international business.

CURRENCY

The United States Dollar has been the official currency since 1973.

TAXATION

There is no income tax or capital gains tax; there is no corporation tax and no turnover or sales tax. No tax is levied on real or personal property and there are no estate duties or inheritance or succession taxes. There is no gift tax and there are no withholding taxes.

There is a nominal Probate Tax with a maximum of $550.00.

The only significant levies which yield revenue to the Government are ad valorem stamp duties (5% of the consideration), on property transactions and also most documentation. There are import duties on goods brought into the Islands at rates ranging between 20-25% depending on whether the goods emanate from the British Commonwealth or from elsewhere. There is also a small departure tax of $3.00 per person.

An "International Company" registered under the International Companies Registration and Certifications Ordinance will enjoy many direct benefits including long term guarantees against possible future taxes both for the company itself and its shareholders. Some of the other privileges and advantages to be enjoyed by an International Company include:-

A. Exemption from taxes, levies, duties and other imposts in respect of the International Company's business activity (the benefit of which will also extend to all beneficial shareholders).

B. Freedom of movement of assets into and from the Islands without the need for consents.

C. Exemption from filing various Returns and Accounts with the International Registrar and freedom from disclosure of beneficial interests and any changes therein.

D. The right to omit the word "LIMITED" on all literature and stationery.

DOUBLE TAX TREATIES

The Islands are not party to any Tax Conventions and are not obliged to comply with a request for information from any overseas Government or Revenue Authority.

EXCHANGE CONTROL

There are no restrictions or controls in force and there is complete freedom of movement of currency and other assets into and out of the Islands.

INVESTMENT AND CAPITAL INCENTIVE SCHEMES

The Government of the Islands actively encourages foreign investment and development. Opportunities are open for overseas investors to establish development of both real estate and commercial enterprises.

TRUST LAW

The Islands do not have any statutes relating to the creation or administration of trusts. These are amply covered by the rules of equity developed

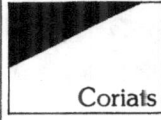

The Games Clan:
Bud, Helen, Ben and Jon
at the Saltraker Inn, GDT
1978

THE PRINCIPALITY'S OLDEST PUB, THE 12-ROOM TURKS HEAD INN, IS THE ORIGINAL WATERING HOLE IN THIS MINI-METROPOLIS. VISITORS WISHING TO JOIN THE RANKS OF WRITERS, DIVERS, COUNTESSES, ECCENTRICS AND INTERESTING PEOPLE WHO FEEL AT HOME IN A SMALL POND SHOULD RESERVE BY PHONE.

GRAND TURK ISLAND, 2466 — OR (312) 763-2007

Welcome to our Islands

85

CALIFORNIA: Europeans brought tiny hitchhikers to the New World—diseases such as smallpox thought to have decimated local populations—that may have changed the climate back home. In soil and sediment data, Stanford scientists found evidence that post-Columbian pandemics led to reforestation as agricultural fields were abandoned. They theorize new plant growth pulled so much carbon dioxide from the air that it contributed to the Little Ice Age, a period of bitter winters between 1550 and 1750.

TURKS AND CAICOS: Slavery had been outlawed in the British Indies by 1841, when the Spanish slave ship *Trouvadore* foundered on a reef off East Caicos Island, so its crew was arrested by authorities. Researchers have now identified the wreck, providing locals with a crucial link to their history—most of the 192 slaves on the ship settled on Grand Turk Island, where a number of African traditions are still practiced.

UK: Archaeologists are studying the remains of the Women's Peace Camp, established to protest the installation of American nuclear weapons at Greenham Common air base. At Turquoise Gate, an offshoot of the main camp started in 1983, they found milk bottles—surprising for a camp that was supposedly vegan—and a doll's torso, like the kind camp residents used to decorate military fences to make them look less threatening and more ridiculous.

CHILE: Agua Buenas was renamed Robinson Crusoe Island in honor of Daniel Defoe's iconic literary castaway. It wasn't arbitrary—Defoe's story is thought to be based on the experience of Alexander Selkirk, a Scottish sailor marooned there from 1704 to 1709. Archaeologists think they have located his campsite—hearths and postholes dating to around the right time—as well as a fragment of what might be a pair of dividers, a tool used for navigation. "Mathematical instruments" were among Selkirk's most prized possessions.

ARGENTINA: One of the birthplaces of the tango—the strutting, sexy partner dance—has been found under Buenos Aires's Palermo Park. The Café de Hansen, established in 1865 and demolished around 1912, was a restaurant and dancehall that hosted tango orchestras as the dance spread from the poor neighborhoods where it began.

CAST

Patriot & Chief Minister of Turks & Caicos Islands

J.A.G.S. McCartney

Montana, GD, Chief of Security the Games Clan

Montana (Guide Dog)

General Manager TCNA the national airline

Ben R. Games, PhD

Deputy Manager TCNA

Loinel Saunders

British Governor of the T & C Islands

Honorable John Strong

Police Commissioner of the Islands

Stanley E. Williams

Friend of JAGS "Super "C"

Earl C. Ingram (PDM

Chief Engineer TCNA

Marsh Greene

Ast. Engineer TCNA

Keith Malcolm

Police Inspector South Caicos

Lightburn

Chief Pilot TCNA

Barkley Barron

T&C Minister of Tourism & Development

Liam Maguire (PDM)

US Treasury Dept Customs Enforcement (Miami)

Dennis R. Fagan

British Caledonia Airlines Director

D.H. (Curly) Walters

Minister of Labor T & C Islands

Hon Lewis Astwood

PDM

Hon Oswald Skippings

PNP

Hon Norman Saunders

Advisor TCNA Comptroller

Helen M. Games, MBA

Advisor TCNA Supply Section

Bud Games, ASS

Ben and Helen Games

AUTHORS PERSONAL INFORMATION

Ben R. Games, PhD, Major, CW-4, TCNA-6, flew bombers and night fighters during WWII. Then Jet Fighters for the USAF during the Korean War, and Chinook helicopters in Vietnam for the 1st Cavalry Division. He is a member of the North American Mach Busters Club and of the Distinguished Flying Cross Society with 737 recorded combat hours. After 35 years he retired from military flying in 1978 and later became the manager of the Turks & Caicos National Airline.

He served in Vietnam as a pilot with the 228 Aviation Battalion, Company B, 1st Cavalry Division, and is a life member of Army Aviation Class 43K, 1st Cavalry Division Association, MOAA, USAF Association, VHPA, DFC

Society, National Guard Association of the US, Camp Grayling Officers Club, VFW, American Legion, and the DAV.

During his military service Ben was awarded the Distinguished Flying Cross for Heroism, Bronze Star, 14 Air Medals, Army Commendation Medal with "V" Device, National Defense Service Medal w/3 Bronze Service Stars, MI Medals of Valor w/Oak leaf cluster, two Legion of Merit. Vietnam Campaign Medal w/1960 device, Republic of Vietnam Gallantry Cross w/Palm Unit Citation, and Republic of Vietnam Civil Actions Medal of Honor with First Class Unit Citation.

During the past fifty years, stories of his adventures have been read by people around the world. They range from a child's Christmas story to biographical adventures to science fiction.

BOOKS WRITTEN: www.FideliPublishing.com

AUTHOR'S BIO

Ben R. Games, PhD, Major, CW-4, TCNA-6

Holds the degrees; Doctor of Philosophy (PhD), Business Administration, Pacific Western University; BS Degrees in; Science, PWU; Nuclear Energy, Air University; Nuclear Disaster Operational Control, USAF; Electronic Engineering, Keio University; Geo-Economics, Notre Dame University; Aviation Pilot Training, Class 43K; Jet Fighter Pilot training, USAF; Radar Navigation training, Victorville AFB; Bombardier School, San Angelo Army Air Field, and Aircraft Accident Investigations, Norton AFB.

Certified Teacher; Basic Flight Training Randolph Field, US Army Air Forces; Instrument Instructor, Texas A&M; Superintendent of Basic Math School, Kessler AFB; Radar Maintenance School, Biloxi, Mississippi; Licensed Insurance Agent #IN64, Airport Manager MI 83-17, Accounting BSc, and Public Health Pest Control #FL 1038.

The author has served on the Board of Directors of the Turks & Caicos National Airlines Inc; H. Jobero Inc an investment firm; Amsie Ltd LLC a building and investment company; Valley Mobilehome Association Inc; Indiana Air Safety Board; and Sabre Service Corporation a legal firm. He co-authored a paper presented to the Aero Medical Lab at Wright Field on the use of pressures instead of vacuums for astronaut training. His doctorate dissertation was on Employer and Employee Relationships Controlled by Governments.

His professional publications included the 1950 secret operational plan for the air defense of the United States, The Independent Worker. Employee Leasing, The Payroll Credit Plan, and Fax/Accounting. Also many of his non-professional books have been read by people all over the world. They are all based on true fact but some are conjecture taken from these facts. He started writing a news column in his Elkhart High School paper in 1942 and continued in 1943 as editor of "Solo" the US Army Primary Class Book of 43K.

For more information or
to purchase books by Ben Games,
visit:

www.FideliPublishing.com

or call
888-343-3542

www.ingramcontent.com/pod-product-compliance
Lightning Source LLC
Chambersburg PA
CBHW071007120726
47910CB00004B/1420